'I wouldn't want to outstay my welcome.'

Jessica moved aside to allow Zac free passage across to the door. She was totally taken by surprise when he pulled her to him to press another pulse-racing kiss to her lips.

'A mouth impossible to resist,' he declared, releasing her again. 'Sweet dreams, green eyes!'

He was gone before she could come up with any kind of reply. As the door closed in his wake her hand crept involuntarily up to touch her lips where the tingle still lingered. She could still smell the faint, emotive scent of his aftershave, still feel the pressure of his body. His departure had left an aching space inside her.

Kay Thorpe was born in Sheffield in 1935. She tried out a variety of jobs after leaving school. Writing began as a hobby, becoming a way of life only after she had her first completed novel accepted for publication in 1968. Since then, she's written over fifty, and lives now with her husband, son, German Shepherd dog and lucky black cat on the outskirts of Chesterfield in Derbyshire. Her interests include reading, hiking and travel.

Recent titles by the same author:

THE ITALIAN MATCH
A MISTRESS WORTH MARRYING
BRIDE ON DEMAND

MISTRESS TO A BACHELOR

BY
KAY THORPE

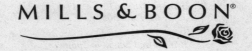

MILLS & BOON and MILLS & BOON with the Rose Device are registered trademarks of the publisher.

First published in Great Britain 2002
Harlequin Mills & Boon Limited,
Eton House, 18-24 Paradise Road, Richmond, Surrey TW9 1SR

© Kay Thorpe 2002

ISBN 0 263 82972 3

Set in Times Roman 10½ on 11½ pt.
01-1002-50577

Printed and bound in Spain
by Litografia Rosés, S.A., Barcelona

CHAPTER ONE

LIGHT as the brush of a butterfly's wings against the sensitive skin at her nape, the kiss brought a dreamy smile to Jessica's lips. She moved instinctively closer to the hard male body at her back, murmuring deep in her throat as a hand slid around her to explore her slender length with a touch like fire, traversing every curve, seeking every intimate crevice, rousing her to an overwhelming need for more.

Paul gave a soft laugh and drew her onto her back to find her lips in a kiss like nothing she had experienced before. Sliding her arms about the broad shoulders, Jessica gave herself up to the embrace, thrilling to the ripple of muscle beneath her fingers.

Since when had Paul had muscles like these? came the sudden thought, snapping her out of the dream and into devastating reality.

Sheer panic propelled her from the bed. 'Who the hell are you?' she demanded.

'I might ask you the same question,' came the answer in tones more intrigued than concerned. 'What happened to Leonie?'

Jessica drew a steadying breath. A stranger to her, but obviously not to Leonie. 'She isn't here.'

Propped on an elbow, the man in the bed reached out a hand to switch on a bedside lamp, playing another, quite different tune on her stomach muscles as she viewed the firm-jawed, assertively masculine features beneath the thick sweep of dark hair.

'I'd rather gathered that,' he said drily. 'It doesn't explain what you're doing in her apartment.'

'I could say the same about—' Jessica caught herself up as he lifted an ironic eyebrow. His reason for being here had to be obvious to all but the densest of mortals.

The gleam of lamplight on his naked shoulders reminded her that the rest of him was naked too. Her breath shortened again at the memory of how it had felt to be held close to that well-honed body—the sensations created by his exploring hands. She should have known the difference the moment he touched her. Paul had never aroused her as fast. Paul had never aroused her to anything like that degree, in fact.

It took the downward drift of steel-grey eyes to bring her to a sudden awareness of the lack of concealment afforded by her semi-sheer nightdress. The cotton wrap she used about the apartment was draped over the end of the bed. She reached for it, steeling herself to ignore the tilt of his lips as she pulled it on.

'Leonie offered me use of the apartment for a break,' she said tautly. 'As you obviously have a key to the place, I'd have thought you'd know her movements.'

The shrug was easy. 'We don't have any hard and fast arrangement. I was driving by and saw the hire car in her parking slot. She doesn't normally let other people use the place.'

'She has this time.' Jessica saw no reason to go into further detail. 'I'd be grateful if you left,' she added with what dignity she could muster. 'You can leave your key on the way out. Leonie can let you have it back when she's next here.'

'Sure.' He came upright, lips quirking once more at the expression on her face as he made to throw back the covers. 'My things are over there on the chair.'

'I'll wait through in the sitting room,' she said hastily.

She made for the door, closing it between the two of them in some temporary relief. Just a few minutes ago she had been on the verge of offering herself with abandonment to a man she didn't know from Adam! Considering her response to him, and his own very obvious arousal, he'd shown considerable strength of mind in managing to treat the situation with any degree of humour at all, she supposed.

The beautifully furnished and decorated room was softly lit by a couple of lamps. He must have switched them on in his progression across to the bedroom. Catching a glimpse of her reflection in the mirror on the wall opposite, Jessica pulled a wry face. With her mop of naturally curly chestnut hair doing its own thing as usual, and her face shining like a beacon from the coating of moisturiser she had given it on retiring, there was little wonder that his passion had died such a swift death.

What she found difficult to understand was Leonie's failure to even mention the fact that someone else had a key to the place. Unless she'd genuinely forgotten about it.

Visualising the man through there in the bedroom, Jessica found that difficult to believe.

It wasn't yet one, she saw from the wall clock. She'd only been asleep an hour or so. Whose bed, she wondered, would Paul be occupying tonight? It was unlikely to be his own.

She thrust the thought from mind as the door behind her opened again, and moved sharply away to turn and confront the man framed in the doorway. He was dressed now in a lightweight pale grey suit and black shirt, the latter open at the neck to reveal a firm tanned throat. Early thirties, she judged, clamping down on the sensations running riot inside her again at the mental image of the body beneath the casual clothing.

'Seems I owe you an apology,' he said with no sign of discomfiture. 'I suppose I should have known.'

'But one woman feels much like another in the dark,' Jessica suggested cynically.

'Only when the body shape's very much the same,' came the smooth response. 'You and Leonie could almost be twins!'

He was laughing at her inwardly if not showing it, Jessica suspected. Eyes like chips of green ice, she said, 'Your key, please!'

'Of course.' He took a key ring from a pocket, and removed one, placing it on the nearest available surface. 'Having got that out of the way, how about a drink before I take to the road again?' he tagged on with what she considered quite astonishing cheek in the circumstances.

'I realise you'll probably be accustomed to having women go to any lengths to keep you around,' she clipped, 'but *I* want you out! You know where the door is.'

'The name's Zac Prescott,' he said, making no move to comply. 'And you are?'

'My name is immaterial. And I don't give a damn who you are! Are you going to leave—or do I have to call the police?'

The firm mouth curved slowly, sensually, sending another warm trickle down her spine. 'To charge me with what? There was no real harm done.'

There might have been, came the unbidden thought, if she hadn't come fully awake in time. The emotion that briefly swept through her was too horrifyingly close to regret for comfort.

'If I hadn't realised *you* weren't who I thought you were, I'm sure you'd have come to your own conclusion before very long,' she retorted.

'Maybe,' he agreed. 'Not to say I'd have had the will-power to stop myself from carrying on regardless though. Whoever you took me for is a lucky man. You're a very responsive lady.'

Jessica felt her colour come up. 'Nothing new for you, I'm sure!'

'Depends on the kind of response we're talking about. You...' He broke off with a smile as she made a vehement gesture in the direction of the door. 'I guess you're right. I wouldn't want to outstay my welcome.'

Jessica moved aside to allow him free passage across to the door. She was taken totally by surprise when he pulled her to him to press another pulse-racing kiss to her lips.

'A mouth impossible to resist,' he declared, releasing her again. 'Sweet dreams, green eyes!'

He was gone before she could come up with any kind of reply. As the door closed in his wake, her hand crept up involuntarily to touch her lips where the tingle still lingered. She could still smell the faint, emotive scent of his aftershave, still feel the pressure of his body. His departure had left an aching space inside her.

Lust, nothing more, she told herself in self-disgust. His physical attraction was undeniable. She supposed she should be grateful he hadn't seen fit to take further advantage of the weakness he must have sensed in her. The experience might have been earth-shaking, but the shame would have haunted her for ever more.

With a return to sleep unlikely until her jangling nerves settled a little, she made herself a cup of coffee and took it out onto the balcony. The sea sparkled silver in the moonlight, the only sign of life a cluster of lights on the horizon. A cruise ship on its way to Palma harbour perhaps.

In a month or so the temperatures would be soaring, but right now the night air felt balmy on her skin. She was to stay as long as she wanted, Leonie had said when offering her use of the apartment. She wouldn't be getting the chance herself this month.

Jessica had seized the opportunity gratefully. A little time on her own was just what she needed in order to get herself back into gear. Looking back, she wondered how she could ever have believed Paul capable of commitment. Men didn't change their inborn habits.

Past *and* done with, she told herself firmly, stifling any pangs. When she left here she would be starting afresh. She had enough put by to see her through until she found a job and somewhere of her own to live. With only her personal possessions to bother about, a bedsit would do for a start. What she wouldn't be doing was taking any more advantage of Leonie's generosity than she absolutely had to.

Back in bed, she still found sleep hard to come by. The masculine scent lingering on the sheets evoked memories she would prefer to forget. There was very little of her that those long supple fingers hadn't explored in those searing moments before realisation had come crashing in.

Zac Prescott. Leonie had certainly never mentioned him. She wondered how long the affair had been going on. It seemed such a casual arrangement. Not that Leonie had ever been what might be called conventional in her way of looking at life. Men, she had often said, were there to be enjoyed for what they were, not castigated for what they were incapable of being.

An attitude, Jessica thought wryly, she might do best to formulate for herself.

Thankfully, she was unlikely to be seeing this particular man again. The very thought of facing those taunting grey eyes was enough to make her squirm.

She slept eventually, waking at seven to the sunlight she was beginning to take for granted. Breakfast out on the balcony was a treat she couldn't have enough of. In daylight the views up and down the rugged western coast-line were spectacular, the detail so clear and sharp at this hour, the air itself like fine wine.

Apart from a couple of trips into Palma, she had taken little advantage of the hire car these past few days. With her return flight booked for the day after tomorrow, it was time she stopped mooning around the apartment and saw something of the rest of the island while she still had the chance. It would be some time before she was able to take another holiday for certain.

She left the small, exclusive apartment block at nine to head up the coast. From her study of the map she had found in the writing desk drawer, she planned on driving as far as Valldemosa, then taking the marked scenic route inland and cutting back across country to hit the main highway again. The heat was rising already, making her glad she had hired one of the canvas-covered jeeps instead of a sedate little saloon.

This early in the season there were relatively few tour-ists on the road. Jessica took her time, stopping at every viewpoint to photograph the stunning coastal and moun-tain scenery. It was coming up to twelve thirty by the time she reached Valldemosa. A good place to have lunch, she decided, her appetite sharpened by the fresh air.

The guidebook she had brought with her gave the Mirador hotel top billing in every sphere. Expensive, of course, but what the hell, Jessica thought recklessly. She was due a little luxury.

Set high up above the lovely mountain village amidst a grove of orange and lemon trees, its white walls clothed in climbing roses and bougainvillaea, the hotel looked to be everything the book said. The jeep safely parked in a corner of the sloping car park, she made her way via a marble-floored, plant-strewn reception area out to a dining terrace overlooking the magnificent panorama.

Even this early in the season, only three of the dozen or so tables were unoccupied. Jessica chose one close by the low parapet wall in order to have an unrestricted view of the scenery, donning her sunglasses against the midday glare. This, she thought luxuriantly, sipping iced orange juice while she perused the extensive menu, was the life! One she could live quite happily given half a chance.

Without lifting her eyes from the menu, she was aware of being studied by the man who was about to take a seat at a nearby table. His scrutiny made her feel uncomfortable. She looked up with what she hoped was a suitably chilling expression when he came over, feeling the bottom drop right out of her stomach as she registered the face she had thought never to see again.

Zac Prescott returned her stunned gaze with an equanimity she only wished she could emulate. 'You turn up in the most unexpected places,' he said.

'I didn't know you were staying here!' Jessica denied, wishing she'd kept her mouth shut as humour sprang in the grey eyes.

'I daresay you'd have steered well clear if you had. But as you are here—' he indicated one of the spare chairs '—perhaps I might join you?'

Jessica vacillated for a lengthy moment, torn between the dictates of common courtesy and the urge to tell him to get lost. Courtesy won by a short head, and only then because of Leonie. 'All right,' she agreed with reluctance.

He pulled out the chair and sat down. His appraisal was too intrusive for comfort. 'You have me at a disadvantage. You know my name but I still have to learn yours.'

'Jessica Saunders,' she acknowledged, unable to come up with any good reason for keeping it a secret.

'Jess for short?'

'Not if you value your health!'

Zac laughed. 'I'll make a note of it.' He studied her again, taking in every detail of her face with its wide-spaced green eyes, small straight nose and soft full mouth. 'I'd say you're a good three or four years younger than Leonie. That would make you around...twenty-five?'

'Almost.' She lifted an eyebrow in faithful imitation of his own interrogative style. 'And you are?'

He laughed again. 'Thirty-three. What's the relationship?' he added. 'You and Leonie, I mean.'

'Why?' she asked.

'Call it plain curiosity. Obviously you don't have to answer.'

What reason was there to keep that a secret either? Jessica asked herself. 'We're cousins,' she said.

'You're in the same line of business?'

It was Jessica's turn to laugh. 'Hardly. I'm just a humble secretary.'

'Secretary maybe, humble I'd doubt,' he returned drily.

He glanced at his watch as a waiter materialised at his elbow, then down at the menu he'd yet to open. 'You go first,' he invited.

'The seafood platter, please,' she said. 'And a Perrier.'

Zac took his time perusing the menu. Crisply styled, the thick dark hair had a healthy shine in the sunlight. From the depth of his tan it seemed evident that he spent a good deal of his time in sunny climates.

Wearing light cotton jeans and a white T-shirt today, he had no less of an impact on her senses; the short sleeves emphasised the muscular structure of his upper arms in a way that made her quiver deep down inside. Last night those arms had enclosed her, those long-fingered hands caressed her. She quivered again at the memory.

She was glad of the dark glasses covering her eyes

when he looked her way again as the waiter departed with their orders. Feeling the way he made her feel was one thing, revealing it quite another.

'Do you spend much time here?' she asked.

'On and off,' he acknowledged. 'Your first visit, is it?'

Jessica nodded. 'It's very different from what I expected.'

'You thought it would be wall-to-wall tourists?'

'More or less.'

'You'd find plenty down around Magaluf, and up the east coast, but this side is too rugged for majority tastes.'

Jessica cast a glance out over the spreading scene. 'It's beautiful! I can understand now why Leonie chose to buy a place here. Not that she gets to use it as often as she'd like these days.'

'The price of success,' Zac observed. 'How long are *you* here for?'

'A week,' she said. 'With two days to go.'

'You think it's going to be long enough to sort yourself out?'

She looked at him sharply, meeting eyes too perceptive by half. 'Sort myself out from what?'

'Whatever it is you're running away from. Could it be the man you mistook me for last night?'

Jessica made every effort to stay cool and collected, if only on the surface. 'Would it really be any of your business?'

'No,' he returned imperturbably, 'but I seem to have struck a chord. Turn out to be a bad lot, did he?'

'Is there any other kind?'

Broad shoulders lifted. 'Don't judge the whole barrel by one rotten apple. Try another.'

'Anyone in mind?' she asked sweetly, and saw his mouth slowly widen.

'I wouldn't say no.'

The sudden flaring temptation was undeniable. Jessica took a forcible hold on herself. Even if the man wasn't her cousin's lover, indulging a purely sexual need was certainly no way to go.

'How long have you known Leonie?' she asked with deliberation.

The question in no way threw him. 'It's a couple of years since we first met, though we only see one another on rare occasions, and never by arrangement. I took the long way up from Palma last night on the off-chance. I planned on surprising her.'

Jessica kept her tone level. 'Sorry to disappoint you.'

'Not so much a disappointment as a deprivation,' he said. 'You were so—'

'I don't want to know!' she cut in hurriedly. 'Just forget about it!'

Zac gave a mock sigh. 'Difficult, but I'll do my best.'

The arrival of the food curtailed conversation for a few minutes. Jessica found the seafood selection delicious—but then for the prices she had seen displayed on the menu, it darn well should be! she reflected. A definite one-off treat.

'So what do *you* do for a living?' she asked lightly.

'I'm with the company contemplating adding this place to their Balearic brochure,' he said.

'The decision dependent on your appraisal?'

'It's certainly a factor.'

Jessica glanced around the wide, tree-shaded terrace. 'It's a lovely place in a wonderful location, though I'd have thought it a bit up-market for the general package deal.'

'It is.' Zac regarded her with new interest. 'Have you worked in the business?'

'Not in the same sense. My parents used to run a hotel in the Cotswolds.'

'Used to?'

'They divorced three years ago.'

'And you joined cousin Leonie in the big city?'

'Not then. I only moved there after…' She caught herself up, aware of having said a great deal more than she had intended. 'Are you considering a recommendation?'

'Maybe.' There was a pause, a change of tone. 'At the risk of being told to mind my own business again, do you still have a job at present?'

Jessica eyed him curiously. 'Why would you want to know?'

'I might be able to put you in the way of something.'

'Are you in the habit of offering jobs to people you only just met?' she asked after a moment.

'No,' he acknowledged.

'Then why me?'

'You're Leonie's cousin, which vouches for your background, and I'm in urgent need of someone available at short notice.' He glanced at his watch again, and pulled a face. 'I'm afraid I have to go. We'll discuss the detail over dinner tonight.'

Pushing back his chair, he stood up, six feet of virile manhood calculated to stir any woman's blood. 'I'll pick you up at eight.'

He strode away before Jessica could draw breath to respond. Not that she was at all sure what she would have said. The offer had come right out of the blue.

An intriguing one, she had to admit. What would prompt a man of his kind to offer any kind of job to someone on the strength of what appeared to be a fairly casual relationship at best?

Listening to what he had to say over dinner in no way committed her, she reasoned. At the very least, she would be spared another long evening on her own. She turned a deaf ear to the voice cautioning against any further association at all with a man who not only sent her pulse rate into overdrive, but made it quite obvious that he found her something of a draw too.

The waiter shook his head when she asked for the bill. Señor Prescott, he said, had already attended to the matter. Jessica wondered if the man knew why Zac was here.

She spent the rest of the afternoon following the lesser frequented route back to her starting point, gaining a glimpse of the real Majorca, almost totally untouched by the tourist trade.

Back at the apartment by five, she made herself coffee, and spent the next hour or so vacillating over whether to ring Leonie or not. The latter was still at the office when she finally made the call.

'You only just caught me,' declared her cousin. 'Another five minutes and I'd have been on my way out for the evening. So, how's it going?'

'Fine,' Jessica assured her. 'I really like the island. What I've seen of it so far, at any rate. I've met a friend of yours,' she went on. 'Name of Zac Prescott?'

There was a pause before Leonie responded. 'Met where exactly?'

Not for anything, Jessica had already decided, was she going to let on about last night, although she doubted if Leonie would find it anything but amusing. 'Valldemosa. The Mirador Hotel. Apparently he works for the company proposing to use the place.'

'Works for?' Leonie gave a laugh. 'Sweetie, he *is* the company. Leastways, a major shareholder. You've heard of Orbis?'

'Vaguely.' Jessica was nonplussed. 'I'd have thought he'd be way above sussing out new prospects?'

'Zac's what you'd call a hands-on man. He hates sitting around in offices. Orbis is one of Prescott Incorporated's subsidiary interests. Caters for the upper end of the travel market. Even more successfully since Zac took it on board.'

Jessica hesitated. 'He's offered me a job.'

'He has?' Leonie sounded taken aback. 'Doing what exactly?'

'I'm not sure yet. I'm having dinner with him tonight to discuss it.'

The response was a moment or two coming. 'I hate to prick any bubbles, but it all sounds a bit pie in the sky.'

'I know.' Jessica kept her tone light. 'No reason why I shouldn't take advantage of an evening out though, is there?'

'Don't go losing your head, that's all. Zac's seduction technique is second to none.'

'I've no intention of losing my head,' Jessica assured her. 'Especially,' she added with purpose, 'over a man you've been having an affair with yourself for two years.'

'No woman lays a claim on Zac Prescott,' came the dry reply. 'He's a totally free spirit. Just take care. You've been through enough over Paul.'

Jessica replaced the receiver, allowing herself no back-sliding in her determination to oust Paul from both heart and mind. Zac's offer of a job might be spurious, but then again it might not. There was only one way she was going to find out.

He arrived at eight on the dot. Wearing off-white trousers and dark tan shirt, he set her pulses hammering the moment he walked through the door. She had a sudden premonition that she was getting into something she would come to regret.

They drove down into Palma for drinks at one of the seafront bars near the cathedral, moving on afterwards to a restaurant overlooking a tree-shaded plaza.

The clientele were clearly of the monied variety, with

a fair scattering of English among them judging from snatches of conversation drifting Jessica's way. Good quality though the natural linen suit she was wearing might be, in her estimation it stood out like a sore thumb among the designer outfits sported by others in the place.

If Zac held the same view, he certainly didn't show it. He'd made no secret of his attraction earlier in the day, and was making no attempt to do so now. As the evening progressed, with no mention of the job he was supposed to be assessing her for, she began to share Leonie's opinion that it might simply have been a means to an end.

There was a part of her, Jessica had to admit, that yearned to just go with the flow and enjoy what her every sense told her would be an experience to remember. Most people her age regarded sexual freedom as a way of life. Why fight the trend?

Because she wasn't most people, came the answer. If Zac really did have designs in that direction, he was going to be very disappointed.

Even more so if she played him along a little, she thought vengefully. He deserved a kick in the teeth.

'I rang Leonie this afternoon,' she said over dessert. 'She tells me you're a company VIP.'

Zac gave her a quizzical look. 'Does it make a difference?'

Her smile was slow. 'Who was it called power an aphrodisiac?'

'Kissinger, I believe.' The grey eyes had acquired a definite glint. 'You reckon he was right?'

'It depends, I suppose, on the way it's handled,' she said. 'Some men are born to it.'

'While others have it thrust upon them. Or is that greatness?' The glint had crystallised into amusement. 'Are you aiming to seduce me?'

'Am I hell!' she exclaimed, abandoning the act. 'You got me here under false pretences!'

Amusement gave way to some other, less discernible expression. 'If you mean the job, you're partially right,' he admitted. 'What I want from you is—'

'Whatever it is, I've no interest,' Jessica cut in. 'Leonie's welcome to you!'

'Leonie isn't here,' he returned. 'Neither would she be right for the part if she were.'

Jessica's brows drew together. 'The part?'

'That's right.' The pause was brief, the grey eyes steady. 'I need a fiancée.'

CHAPTER TWO

JESSICA gave a derisive laugh. 'If that's meant to be a joke of some kind, it's a pretty poor effort!'

'I'm not joking.' Zac spoke quite calmly. 'I'll pay you a thousand to pretend to be my fiancée.'

He really was serious, she realised, studying him. Her first inclination was to tell him where he could go with his preposterous proposal, but curiosity held a stronger hand.

'Just what kind of game are you playing?' she demanded.

'No game,' he assured her. 'I let my grandfather believe I'd found the girl of my dreams at last. Now he wants to meet her.'

'Why?' she asked in some confusion. 'I mean, why tell him something that obviously isn't true?'

'Because it stopped him pressuring me to get married and start a family for a while.'

'A state you'd naturally abhor.' Jessica made no attempt to eradicate the sarcasm from her voice. 'Hardly likely to be a very long-lasting deception, was it?'

Broad shoulders lifted. 'So I didn't think too far ahead at the time.'

'Then why not just tell him the truth and have done with it?'

'Because he only has a short time to live.' Zac's tone was flat. 'And before you ask, I only found out this morning. I can't spring it on him now. Hence the desperate straits.'

'I doubt if you'd find any shortage of takers if you rang around.'

'Not in the time. You're my only hope.'

Jessica regarded him in silence for several seconds, grappling with the implications. To do what he was asking her to do would be shameful, but if the alternative meant robbing a dying man of his dearest wish…

'It's emotional blackmail!' she accused.

'I'm aware of it.' He studied her set features. 'If a thousand isn't enough…'

Green eyes flared. 'If I do it at all, it certainly won't be for money!' She looked at him with distaste. 'I hope you're proud of yourself!'

'Not over this,' he admitted. 'I just wanted breathing space. Time to find a woman I could contemplate living with full time.'

'The main problem might be finding one who could contemplate living with *you* full time!' Jessica retorted, bringing a tilt to his lips.

'Quite possibly.'

But unlikely, she was bound to admit. No man with Zac Prescott's assets would have difficulty finding a wife.'

'I'd have thought Leonie might fulfil your every requirement in that direction,' she said.

'Leonie?' He laughed, shaking his head. 'She'd no more want to marry me than I would her. We're too much alike.'

'Opposites attract, similarities endure,' she murmured.

'Sometimes, not always.'

'So what would you consider ideal wife material? Someone who'd hang on your every word and worship the ground you walked on?'

The scorn made little impression. 'Sounds pretty close.'

'You're about fifty years too late then.'

'So it seems.' Zac shook his head again, this time in

mock despair. 'I might have to settle for less than the best in the end.'

'Whoever you did marry would have my heartfelt sympathy!' It was weak, but the best she could come up with.

'I'll pass the message on, if and when,' he said. 'To get back to the lesser proposal, if you won't take money, how about that job? Obviously it wouldn't be with Prescotts, but I have plenty of contacts.'

Jessica curled a lip. 'Don't bother. I'll be doing it for one reason and one reason only, and that's to save your grandfather from knowing what a liar you are!'

'Thanks.' Zac neither sounded nor looked in any way discomposed by the censure. 'So we'd better get down to discussing detail. I've worked out a potted history for you. All you have to do is memorise it.'

'Taking it for granted I was going to say yes?'

The grey eyes remained steady. 'You can learn a lot about someone in a very short time in bed.'

Jessica felt the contraction deep in the pit of her stomach, the sudden wave of heat through her body. 'You know nothing about me!' she exclaimed furiously, colouring afresh at the memory of those exploring hands. 'Nothing intrinsic, at any rate. I can still back out. What would you do then?'

'I'd be sunk,' he admitted. 'But you won't back out.'

He was right, she conceded with reluctance. However much she might deplore the situation, she'd committed herself.

'It will be easier if I use my own background,' she said, with no intention of relinquishing at least that much control.

'No reason why not,' he agreed after a moment's consideration. 'Probably easier for me too, in fact. I'll need a few more details though.'

'I think you'd better fill *me* in on a few details first. Where exactly is your grandfather, to start with?'

'Dorset. Near Lyme Regis. They moved down there when he retired.'

Jessica looked at him sharply. 'They?'

'He and my grandmother.' Zac raised a querying eyebrow. 'Does it make a difference?'

'It means deceiving two people instead of one—unless you plan on telling your grandmother the truth.'

'I think she might have enough on her plate for the time being, don't you?'

Jessica had to agree with that too. The arrival of a waiter to exchange the unfinished desserts for coffee gave her a much needed break. She took hers strong and black in an attempt to clear her mind.

'You said you only heard the news this morning?' she queried when they were alone again.

Zac nodded. 'Grandmother told me when I rang to say I wouldn't be able to make it this weekend.'

'The news must have been a real shock.'

A shadow passed over the incisive features. 'Very much so. I knew he was on medication for angina, and, at eighty, I suppose it was on the cards that he might not have all that long, but I just didn't expect it this soon.'

He briskened his tone, emotions under firm control again. 'I haven't given them a name as yet, so your own will do.'

Jessica held back the acrid comment. 'How long are we supposed to have known one another?'

'A couple of weeks or so.'

'Obviously love at first sight!'

The satire lit a spark in his eyes. 'It happens to others, why not to me?'

'You're hardly the type.'

'I'm no out-and-out romantic, I agree, but I'm not quite as case-hardened as you seem to think.'

'I'll take your word for it. I already told you as much of my background as you really need to know about for now,' Jessica went on purposefully, caught up, despite her disquietude, in the concoction. 'Where did we meet?'

Zac gave a brief shrug. 'At a party?'

'You've really thought this through, haven't you?' she gibed.

'Not to any great extent,' he admitted. He studied her for a moment, expression undecipherable. 'You're being very...cooperative.'

'For your grandfather's sake, not yours. One thing we should have clear,' she added, arming herself against any intruding images, 'there'll be no physical contact between us.'

The spark was lit once more. 'It's hardly going to be convincing if I'm banned from even putting an arm around you.'

'No more than strictly necessary then.'

'Who is it you mistrust the most?' he asked softly. 'Me—or yourself?'

Both equally, if she were honest, Jessica could have told him. However she might feel about his behaviour in this particular matter, there was no getting away from her physical responses.

She met his gaze with what she hoped was a suitably scathing expression. 'Modesty not exactly your strong point, is it?'

'Attack the best means of defence?' he countered. 'Why do some women find it necessary to deny their natural leanings? It isn't essential to be in love to get pleasure from love-making. I'd have thought last night would have proved that to you.'

'We were hardly together long enough to prove *any-*

thing,' Jessica retorted, knowing even as she said it that she was fighting a losing battle. 'When exactly do you plan on seeing your grandfather?' she asked, thrusting the thought aside.

'As soon as possible. If we can't get a scheduled flight tomorrow, I'll book a charter. We'll be going straight down to the house, which means an overnight stay. Separate rooms, so you'll be safe enough. Grandmother would have it no other way.'

Neither, it was on the tip of Jessica's tongue to retort, would she. She refrained because it was more dignified to ignore the comment. 'What about the rest of your family? Will they be there too?'

'What's left of it. My father and his brother were killed together in a car crash seven years ago.' The statement was matter-of-fact.

'I'm sorry,' Jessica proffered. 'It must have been hard.'

'It was.' Zac glanced at the thin gold watch encircling one lean wrist, face revealing little. 'More coffee, or shall we make tracks?'

It was coming up to midnight, Jessica saw from her own watch. Looking back over the evening, she could still hardly believe what she'd agreed to do. Leonie would consider her a total idiot for getting involved in such a scheme. She wouldn't be far wrong either.

'I'm ready to go,' she said. 'I hadn't realised it was so late.'

His smile had a sardonic edge. 'Time flies when you're having fun.'

It was a short walk to where they'd left the car. Although nowhere near as busy as it would be in months to come, the town was humming with activity, the night only just getting into its stride.

Aware through every nerve and sinew of the man at her side, Jessica took care to keep space between them.

Had she been with Paul right now, came the thought, he would have wanted to visit at least one nightclub before retiring. She was surprised by the lack of any real pain in the memory. Perhaps her feelings for him hadn't gone quite as deep as she'd imagined after all.

The drive back was accomplished in near silence. Jessica was thankful not to be the one tackling the steep climbs and hairpin bends in the dark. Zac insisted on seeing her as far as the main door of the apartments, though he made no attempt to solicit an invitation.

'I'll be here at nine,' he said. 'You can leave your car. I'll arrange to have it picked up. Hopefully, we'll be in England by mid-afternoon.' Catching the expression that flitted across her face, he added hardily, 'You're not going to let me down.'

It was more of a statement than a question, but this was no time, Jessica acknowledged, to be nitpicking over inflections.

'I'll be ready,' she said. 'Although I can't pretend to be happy about what we're doing. I hope you can live with yourself afterwards.'

'I'll do my best.' He paused. 'Are you planning on telling Leonie about it?'

'I'd as soon *no* one else knew about it!'

'Supposing she tries to get in touch with you?'

'I'll ring her first thing in the morning and tell her I'm going to spend a few days on the other side of the island,' she said. 'What's one more lie?'

Zac's face remained impassive. 'See you at nine, then.'

Jessica closed the door, watching through the glass as he strode back to the car, tall, lean and totally devastating. She had given her word. No going back. Whatever the outcome, she would deal with it.

Morning found her with certain misgivings still, but no lessening of resolve. A dying man's peace of mind took precedence over conscience.

Allowing for the time difference, she waited until eight to put through the call to Leonie, only to have the other call her first.

'So how did it go last night?' asked her cousin without preamble. 'Did you get the job?'

Jessica put everything she had into keeping her voice from revealing her inner turbulence. 'There was no job. You were right about him. He had a hidden agenda.'

The pause was loaded. 'Did you...?'

'Succumb?' Jessica forced a short laugh. 'Give me credit for a little sense!'

'Sense doesn't play all that large a part in some situations,' came the dry reply. 'Don't try telling me he leaves you totally cold.'

Denials would be a waste of breath, Jessica knew. She opted for cynicism instead. 'I admit he's got something, but hell will freeze over before I let my hormones rule me again. Anyway, I'd hardly want to trample on your preserves.'

'I already told you, Zac's a free spirit.' Leonie sounded cynical herself. 'The only reason I warned you against him was because I didn't want you falling for him on the rebound. I take it you'll not be seeing him again?'

Jessica steeled herself against the urge to confess all, knowing all too well what her cousin would say. 'No. As a matter of fact, I was thinking of changing my flight and spending a few days over the other side of the island.'

'Good idea,' Leonie agreed. 'Make the most of it while you can. See you when you get back.'

She didn't wait for any response, which was fortunate as Jessica would have been hard put to it to hit the right note. Deceiving her cousin was not something she liked doing, but there was no way she could bring herself to tell her the truth.

Her bag packed, she was ready and waiting in a dark cream trouser suit when Zac arrived promptly on the hour. He gave her a deliberated scrutiny, meeting her eyes with a smile on his lips.

'You look perfect. Grandmother will love the curls. I find them pretty appealing myself, if it comes to that.'

Jessica gave him a less than appreciative look, disregarding the impact he made in the same pale grey suit he had worn the other night, this time with a dull gold shirt. 'You don't need to start playing the part yet.'

'Just getting the feel of it,' he responded. 'I'd doubt if Grandfather's mind is any less astute than it ever was.'

'There'll come a time when you have to come clean,' she pointed out. 'To your grandmother, at least.'

'I'll cross that bridge when I come to it.' Zac made an abrupt movement. 'Let's go.'

He carried her bag down to the car and stowed it in the boot alongside his own, then saw her into the passenger seat. Jessica stopped herself from moving away when he slid in behind the wheel, but only just. Relatively spacious though the car interior was, he was still too close for comfort. The clean fresh tang of his aftershave tantalised her nostrils.

The car had air-conditioning, but Jessica had no quarrel with Zac's preference for open windows. She took off her jacket and tossed it to join his on the back seat, enjoying the cool rush of air on her bare arms. Cut to follow the shape of her body without undue clinging, the sleeveless, emerald green top drew a frankly appraising glance, making her wish she'd kept the jacket on. The last thing she'd want was for him to think she was flaunting herself.

'You said your grandfather was eighty,' she remarked,

looking for something—anything—to talk about. 'Is your grandmother younger?'

'The same, within a couple of months. They grew up next door to one another.' Zac gave a dry smile. 'I'd say their fates were sealed from an early age.'

'Do they know we're coming?'

'I rang last night to say we'd be there for dinner.'

Jessica gave him a surprised glance. 'But it must have been going up the hill for two by the time you got to the hotel.'

'I meant earlier.' There was no element of apology in his tone. 'A calculated gamble.'

'Do you take chances in business affairs too?' she queried after a moment.

'On occasion. Playing it safe all the time makes for a very dull life. I haven't fallen on my face yet.'

'There's always a first time,' Jessica retorted. 'Your grandfather still has to be convinced.'

'He will be.'

She looked out of the side window, hoping he was right. To be caught out in a lie of this magnitude at such a time was beyond contemplation.

They were at the airport by ten fifteen. Zac, it turned out, had already phoned through before leaving the hotel, and managed to book two seats on a scheduled flight leaving at midday. Jessica took the time to cancel her reservation on the following day's flight, accepting the lack of refund due to short notice as a matter of course. Right now it was a minor consideration.

Flying first class was an event in itself. Cocooned in soft leather comfort, a glass of champagne at her elbow, Jessica was forced to concede the advantages. If the engagement was for real, this was the kind of lifestyle she would be living from now on. Few people could honestly claim to find nothing appealing in that notion.

Only it wasn't for real. Once the weekend was over, she and Zac would go their separate ways—with any subsequent fallout from the deception his problem. The fact that she was going to find him difficult, if not downright impossible, to forget was *her* problem. How did one go about forgetting a man who set every nerve ending on fire?

She stole a glance at him, relaxed in his seat, head back against the rest, eyes closed. The firm lines of his mouth aroused an aching desire to know its touch again; she felt her nipples spring to life at the very thought. A weakness she'd better get a hold on if she was to emerge from this encounter with some shred of self-respect left, she told herself hardily.

Zac had a car at Heathrow. By two o'clock English time, they were on the road.

After a week of warm sun, the pouring rain was hardly scheduled to lift any spirits. Jessica found hers sinking ever deeper as the miles went by. However good the intention, she was entering into a conspiracy to deceive a dying man. If Zac himself felt no shame, she certainly did.

'I'm not sure I can go through with this,' she said.

Zac gave her a swift glance, his jaw firming. 'You can't back out now!'

'You can't *make* me carry on with it!' she responded.

'Not physically, perhaps. But ethically you're...'

'You're a fine one to talk about ethics!' Jessica shot back. 'If you hadn't lied in the first place, none of this would be necessary!'

'I'm aware of it. As time travel isn't yet possible, unfortunately, we're all of us stuck with the mistakes we make. You agreed to do this for my grandfather's sake, not mine. He's the one you'd be letting down.'

Jessica bit her lip. 'All right. I'll do my best.'

'Thanks.' His tone had softened. 'You're one in a million, Jess!'

For once she allowed the shortening of her name to pass. There were far more important things to think about.

It was coming up to six o'clock when they finally reached their destination. Lying a couple of miles from the coast, Whitegates turned out to be a converted nineteenth-century farmhouse set within several acres of land. Getting from the car on the wide fronting driveway, Jessica stood for a moment to view the place, loving its timelessness, its air of tranquillity.

'Not what you were expecting?' asked Zac, moving back to open the boot.

'I hadn't actually thought about it,' she admitted. 'I suppose if I had, I might have imagined something built to order.'

'More suited to a retired elderly couple?'

'Well...yes. This is wonderful, but it must be a lot of work.'

'A fair amount,' he agreed. 'But help isn't too much of a problem. They have a daily maid-cum-cook, plus a whole army of cleaners, gardeners, whatever, to call on.'

Silly of her to think otherwise considering the family background, Jessica reflected. Finances would hardly be strained.

The woman who appeared at the top of the steps leading up to a side door fitted no conventional grandmother image for certain. Tall and slim in a pair of tailored blue trousers and matching shirt, her silvered hair superbly cut to frame her face, she looked nowhere near her age.

'I was beginning to wonder if you were ever going to get here,' she said. The smile she gave Jessica was strained. 'It's so nice to meet you at last.'

'I'm only sorry it had to be under these circumstances,' Jessica rejoined, hating herself for her part in this travesty—hating Zac even more at the moment for involving her in the first place.

'Where is Grandfather?' asked Zac.

'In the sitting room waiting for you.' The faded blue eyes appraised the bags he was carrying, lingering on Jessica's so much larger suitcase. 'How long are you planning on staying?'

'No set plan.' Zac ignored Jessica's swift glance. He pressed a kiss to his grandmother's cheek. 'How's he taking it?'

To Jessica, the expression that flickered across the older woman's face was more reminiscent of discomfiture than distress. Her tone when she answered was oddly evasive.

'As he takes everything. He's very much looking forward to seeing you both.' The pause was brief. 'He'd prefer you didn't mention his condition. Just treat him as normal.'

The side door led directly into a big stone-floored kitchen. Apart from the dark green Aga range fitted into a wide recess that had probably once been the fireplace, the room was unmodernised, with solid old cupboards and dressers, its rough plastered walls painted a deep warm terracotta. Exposed beams ran across the ceiling.

The woman preparing vegetables at one of the two Belfast sinks looked round with a smile at their entry.

'Nice to see you again, Mr Zac.' The glance she cast Jessica's way was frankly curious. 'Congratulations to you both!'

Zac returned the smile. 'Thanks. Jessica, meet Dulcie.'

Jessica made a suitable acknowledgement of both introduction and wishes, gearing herself for what was still to come. She felt terrible again already, and this was only the beginning. The thought of facing a dying man with the same lies on her lips made her want to throw up.

They left the bags where Zac had dropped them, and

followed his grandmother across a wide hall to a beamed sitting room beautifully furnished and decorated in period. The figure stretched out on a sofa beneath one of the mullioned windows appeared to be sleeping. Lean in build, with a full head of white hair above a thin but by no means emaciated face, he looked far from the frail old man Jessica had been anticipating.

'Don't waken him,' she said impulsively as Mrs Prescott reached to touch his shoulder. 'He must need all the sleep he can get.'

She was too late. He was already opening his eyes. Grey eyes, like his grandson's, though lacking the steely clarity. She found a smile as they locked onto her face.

'Hello, Mr Prescott. I'm Jessica.'

'Welcome to the family, Jessica,' he said, with none of the confusion that might be expected of someone just woken from sleep. 'I've waited a long time for this.'

'Let Zac help...' she began as he made to lever himself upright, breaking off as she recalled his wife's injunction.

'I don't need cosseting,' he rejoined without particular inflection.

His wife looked as if she was about to make some comment, spreading her hands in a dismissive gesture as he gave her a frowning glance. 'Pull up a chair for the girl, Zac,' he commanded.

Zac did so, face revealing little of what was going on inside his head. Jessica could only hope his guilt was eating him up to the same degree.

'So tell me about yourself,' the old man invited. 'You've certainly got the looks I'd have expected, but there has to be more to you than that to throw a noose round this grandson of mine.'

Jessica shook herself inwardly. Dying he might be, easy to fool he most certainly wasn't. She was going to need all her wits about her to make this convincing.

'I've no hidden depths,' she disclaimed. 'What you see is what you get.'

The chuckle was unexpected. 'I'll form my own judgement. So, how did the two of you meet?'

Forward planning certainly paid off, came the fleeting thought. 'At a party,' she said.

'You were drawn to one another across a crowded room, eh?'

She gave a laugh, drawing on her imagination. 'Actually, we ran into one another—literally—dancing. I put a heel in Zac's instep, so it was hardly what you'd call an auspicious beginning.'

'It obviously made an impression on him.'

'Like being poleaxed!' Zac's tone was light. 'I've been out of circulation ever since.'

'One good woman is worth a thousand of the other kind,' his grandfather rejoined. 'You've sown enough wild oats.'

'A man must do what a man must do,' Jessica observed blandly, opting for a bold approach. 'I daresay you did some sowing of your own before you met your wife.'

'I was married at twenty,' he said.

She bit her lip. 'I'm sorry.'

'No need.' He was obviously enjoying her discomfiture. 'How about you? Ever been in love before?'

Jessica met the shrewd gaze head on. 'I might have thought I was.'

'But you know the difference now?'

In for a penny, in for a pound! she thought, unable to prevaricate her way around a straight question. She softened both voice and expression. 'Oh, yes!'

Henry Prescott had subsided back into the cushions, though not, it was apparent, with the intention of drifting off to sleep again.

'What about family?' he asked.

'My parents are divorced,' she said, reconciling herself to the inevitable. 'Both of them remarried.'

'I see.' He sounded disapproving. 'Brothers and sisters?'

'No, I was an only child. Fate,' she added, sensing the question before it was asked, 'not choice. They'd have liked a son.' Preferred would have been a better word, though she doubted if even that would have saved a marriage destined from almost the start not to run its full course. 'I live in London now.'

Would be doing, at any rate, once this was over, she thought.

'And what do you do *for* a living?'

Her hesitation was brief. 'Secretarial.'

'You'll be giving it up, of course, once you and Zac are married.'

It was a statement not a question. Easy to see where his grandson got it from, thought Jessica drily. 'I hadn't got round to thinking about it yet,' she said.

The old eyes bored into her. 'But you do want children?'

'Well…yes.' Don't just stand there! she thought fumingly when there was no word from Zac. 'Four at least,' she tagged on, throwing caution to the winds. 'Two boys, two girls, if we can manage it.'

There was a certain satisfaction in the look Henry Prescott turned his grandson's way. 'It took you long enough, but it seems you might have made it good in the end.'

'Didn't I just,' Zac agreed.

Jessica concentrated on her glass, conscience overtaking her once more. She was never going to forgive herself for this! They'd been here less than half an hour. The thought of keeping the act going until at least lunchtime tomorrow was daunting.

CHAPTER THREE

ZAC stayed for a few private words with his grandfather while his grandmother showed Jessica to the room she would be occupying. Furnished to suit the ambience of the place, it boasted a small but beautifully appointed en suite.

'You have a lovely home, Mrs Prescott,' Jessica exclaimed impulsively. 'So unspoiled!'

'It would have been a crime to make changes other than what was strictly necessary,' the older woman agreed. 'I see you're not wearing a ring yet,' she added disconcertingly.

'We didn't get round to choosing one yet,' Jessica improvised. 'It's all happened so quickly. I'm still having difficulty taking it in!'

'It came as a surprise to Henry and me too. We were beginning to believe Zac would never settle down. Henry regards marriage as the mainstay in a man's life. To the right woman, of course. As you might have gathered, he doesn't approve of working wives. Not outside the home, at any rate. He wouldn't have been at all happy if you'd turned out to be career-minded.'

Jessica bit back the instinctive rejoinder. 'You never had any ambition in that direction yourself?' she asked instead.

'I never had the opportunity to develop that kind of ambition. Not that I believe I missed out in any way.'

The rider had been added a little too quickly for complete conviction, Jessica thought. Here was a woman who had known at least some degree of frustration with her lot over the years.

'I'm not sure I could settle for domesticity wholesale,' she said lightly. 'I doubt if Zac would expect it of me anyway.'

'He'll need to give the impression he not only expects it but insists on it if he wants to stay in his grandfather's good books,' came the candid reply. 'Henry is capable of settling the majority of his company shares on our other grandson if Zac proves himself less than the man he hopes he is. Not something I personally...'

Esther Prescott broke off, shaking her head as if in the realisation of already having said a great deal more than she had intended. 'Do make yourself at home,' she substituted. 'We live a very informal life here.'

Alone in the room, Jessica tried to bring her thoughts into some kind of order. If Zac knew his grandfather's views, and he must surely do, he'd taken a grave risk in coming up with this pseudo fiancée to start with. Playing for time, he'd said last night, but time had run out on him faster than he'd anticipated.

With so much to possibly lose, there was small wonder for the desperation stakes, she reflected cynically. She could have gone along with the 'pacifying a dying man' theme—she *had* gone along with it—but this was something else again. Zac deserved to be exposed for what he was!

But was she prepared to do it? she asked herself. Could she bring herself to tell a dying man that his grandson had lied to him simply to stay in favour?

The answer had to be no. Which left her with little recourse but to carry on with the deception for the time being, like it or not.

Zac gave her a questioning look when he brought in

her suitcase a few minutes later, obviously picking up on the vibes.

'Something wrong?'

'I let myself be talked into this to spare your grandfather the distress of knowing you'd lied to him,' she jerked out. 'But that wasn't all *you* were worried about, was it? You were afraid of him changing his will if he found you out!'

The hard-boned face showed little expression. 'It was a consideration, yes. He can be quite ruthless.'

'Something you should maybe have thought about before putting on the act in the first place!'

'True,' he agreed with maddening calm. 'Call it a momentary aberration.'

'You really don't give a damn about anything or anyone but yourself, do you?' she accused. 'In fact, the sooner your grandfather dies, the better for you!'

It didn't need the sudden flare in the grey eyes to tell her she had gone too far. 'I'm sorry,' she said thickly. 'That was a lousy thing to say!'

'If it's what you think, why bottle it up?' he rejoined.

'It isn't.' Jessica paused in some confusion. 'At least, not quite to that extent.'

'It just came out under pressure?' Zac suggested on an ironical note. 'Rather different circumstances, maybe, but I know the feeling.' He studied her, expression unreadable again. 'So, what's the decision? Are you going to insist I tell him the truth?'

'How can I?' she said. 'There's no knowing what it might do to him. We'll just have to carry it through. Just don't try taking advantage, that's all.'

'I'll do my best to keep my distance.'

Jessica shot a glance at him, infuriated once more to see the faint smile hovering about his lips.

'I see nothing even remotely funny about this!' she snapped.

'Me neither,' he agreed. 'But better a smile than a frown. However much I might regret it, what's done is done. Wallowing in guilt isn't going to help.'

Reluctant though she was to acknowledge it, he was right, she supposed. If there was to be no confession, they were left with no choice other than to continue the sham. With conviction too if his grandfather wasn't to begin suspecting something.

'You've told him we're only here until tomorrow?'

'Not in so many words.'

Jessica hardened both heart and voice. 'Have you given any thought at all to what you'll do if he asks to see the pair of us again?'

'Another bridge to cross if and when necessary.' His gaze roved her face, his lips twisting. 'A pity it has to end like this.'

'It never started,' she retorted, steeling herself against the response he could still draw from her. 'I'll be *ecstatically* happy never to see you again!'

Humour sprang briefly in the grey eyes. 'A little overstated for total conviction, but I get the message.'

Jessica turned away, unable to sustain the degree of anger that had kept her going these last minutes. An anger which, she had to admit, had been directed as much at herself for her inability to repress the emotions he aroused in her still. Tomorrow couldn't come soon enough!

Henry Prescott ate sparingly at dinner, though he enjoyed a glass of wine. Watching him surreptitiously, listening to him talk, Jessica found it difficult to believe he was even as old as he was, much less on the verge of dying.

'We're usually in bed by ten o'clock,' said Esther over

coffee, 'but you mustn't feel you have to retire then your-selves.'

'Just try not to waken us when you do come up,' said her husband. 'At our age, we need our beauty sleep.'

'You neither of you look your age,' Jessica commented, and drew an appreciative smile.

'I'd like to say I don't feel it either, but it wouldn't be entirely true. You must make sure you have your children while you're still young and fit. This modern idea of wait-ing until middle age is abominable! I had my two sons by the time I was twenty-three.'

His two sons, Jessica noted. She stole a glance at his wife, expecting to see some sign, however faint, of re-sentment, but her face was devoid of expression.

'We're a bit late getting away from the starting post,' said Zac easily, 'but we'll do our best.'

'Good.' His grandfather looked from one to the other. 'So, when's the wedding to be?'

Jessica drew in a long slow breath. It should have been a foregone conclusion that the question would be asked at some point, but it hadn't even crossed her mind until this moment.

'Soon,' Zac answered.

'How soon?' Henry insisted. 'I'd like to be around for it.'

Esther made a sound as if about to say something, shak-ing her head as he gave her a sharp glance. It was left to Zac to fill the silence.

'Weddings take time to arrange. We didn't even set a date yet.'

'Then it's high time you did.' The older eyes were un-yielding. 'What reason is there to wait if you know your minds?'

Jessica sent Zac an urgent signal via a foot under the table. There was no way they were going to get out of this other than admitting to the whole fabrication, so best to just get on with it and face the consequences.

Zac gave no sign of even feeling the kick. 'No reason at all,' he said. 'We'll set things in motion.'

'Good,' his grandfather said again. His gaze shifted to Jessica. 'You've no objection, I take it?'

She had every objection, but no nerve to voice them. Calling all kinds of curses down on Zac's head, she managed a creditably steady answer in the negative. This was one bridge he would definitely be crossing on his own. Once away from here, she was out of it!

There was no further talk of weddings, to her relief, but she found it far from easy to act naturally. Zac appeared completely at ease. The hallmark of a born con man, she thought wrathfully.

She refrained from immediate comment when the Prescotts departed, seeking just the right words. Zac forestalled her.

'Get it off your chest,' he advised drily. 'Then we can decide where we go from here.'

'There's no going anywhere from here!' she snapped back, losing track of the flak she'd been about to turn out. 'You *have* to tell them the truth!'

'You think that wise?' he asked after a moment.

'I think it quite likely you could lose your precious shares, but I doubt if it will kill him outright.'

'There's no certainty of it though. He has little enough time left as it is. Would you want to be responsible for adding to the stress?'

Jessica was silent for a lengthy moment. When she spoke again her voice sounded strained. 'So, what's *your* proposal?'

'Just let it ride for now.'

'Where will that get you if he lives longer than ex-

pected?' she asked. 'And don't say you'll cross that bridge
if and when necessary, or I swear I'll hit you!'

'I won't, then.'

Jessica glanced at him suspiciously, sensing a certain
lack of gravity in his voice. 'I must have been mad letting
you talk me into any of this!'

'Not mad,' he declared. 'Just exceptionally charitable.
I can't think of anyone else who would have agreed to do
what you're doing unconditionally.'

'Some would have been prepared to take money for it?'

'I reckon I might have been called on to offer a great
deal more than that.'

'A real engagement rather than a spurious one, you
mean?' Jessica gave a short laugh. 'I'm sure you're considered quite a catch, but a woman would have to be
pretty desperate to take that kind of advantage.'

'You might be surprised by the lengths some will go
to when it comes to securing a comfortable future.'

'You've been mixing with the wrong type then!'

'There could be some truth in that. Your cousin aside,'
he added. 'Leonie regards marriage the same way I've
always seen it up to now, as something to be avoided at
all costs.'

'So all that talk last night about gaining breathing space
to find a woman you could contemplate sharing your life
with was so much hogwash!' Jessica berated.

'I said up to now. Given the right woman, it might be
possible to make something worthwhile out of it.' He
slanted a glance. 'Fancy giving it a try?'

'I'd as soon jump off a cliff!'

The sigh was exaggerated. 'You're probably right. I'd
make a lousy husband!'

The flickering glow from the log fire crackling in the
wide stone hearth highlighted the firm masculine features,
bringing an all too familiar tension in the region of her

stomach. Two nights ago they had shared a bed. At this precise moment she could think of nothing else but the muscular feel of him. Whatever her views on his conduct, there was no denying the need he aroused in her.

He knew it too, if the expression in the grey eyes was anything to go by.

'Electrifying, isn't it?' he said softly. 'The question is, what are we going to do about it?'

Making out she didn't know what he was talking about was pointless, Jessica acknowledged. He knew exactly what was in her mind.

'Absolutely nothing,' she said flatly. 'After tomorrow you're on your own. I don't want to see you or hear from you again.'

His smile was slow. 'You don't lie very well.'

'It's the truth.' She did her best to keep both voice and expression impassive. 'As Leonie won't be expecting me back for a day or two I'll have to check into a hotel for a couple of nights at least. You can pay for that, but nothing more.'

'And after?' he prompted.

'I'll be staying with Leonie while I look for a job.'

'No secretarial position alone is ever going to satisfy you,' Zac declared. 'You need a challenge in life.'

'You've no idea what I need!' she retorted, drawn despite herself.

'Yes, I do.' There was a wicked light in his eyes. 'You're a vibrant, passionate woman aching for the same thing I'm aching for myself right now.'

Jessica was slow to react as he reached for her. The hands curving her upper arms were firm in their grasp though in no way hard, the kiss a heart thudding, stomach curling, totally irresistible force.

Her response was instinctive, all thought temporarily suspended. His mouth was a source of endless pleasure, the silky slide of his tongue between her lips no intrusion. She tremored as the long tensile fingers lightly traced the curve of her breast.

She came to her senses with a jerk. Zac made no move to detain her as she thrust herself away from him.

'This has to stop!' she breathed.

'You're not going to try making out it's all one-sided,' he said softly.

Grateful for the dim light, Jessica made a supreme effort to bring her emotions under control. Her voice sounded steadier at least. 'Obviously not, but this is as far as it goes. I'm here for the one purpose, and one purpose only! After tomorrow, that's it!'

'It doesn't have to be,' he said. 'We could see how things go.'

'I know exactly how things would go,' she declared. 'The same way I imagine all your affairs go! Thank you, ma'am, and goodbye!'

'Succinct—' he grinned '—but not true. I've never had any interest in one-night stands.'

'Which category does Leonie come under?'

'Leonie comes under her own category. She certainly has no proprietorial instincts, if that's what's worrying you.'

'In two years, you must have slept together on a fair number of occasions.'

'With long gaps in between.'

'And you think I'd be prepared to help fill in the gaps?'

'That isn't what I have in mind.' His gaze roved her face, lingering on the provocative fullness of her mouth. Voice roughened, he said, 'I want you, Jess!'

The abbreviation of her name failed to irk her; she was too intent on trying to keep her feet on the ground. 'Why?' she asked huskily.

'Why?' His regard was quizzical. 'Because you've been

driving me wild since we met. Because you're an out-standingly attractive young woman with far more than just your looks about you. Whoever Paul is, he isn't worth putting your life on hold over. You need to move on.'

'I already did.'

'Not far enough. I could make you forget him.'

Her lips twitched involuntarily. 'You're certainly not lacking in confidence!'

'Would you like me better if I was backward in coming forward?'

'I'm unlikely to find out.'

'The love of a good woman could make a new man of me,' he said with mock gravity.

'Leopards don't change their spots,' she rejoined.

'Black ones don't have any to start with.' Zac was silent for a moment. When he spoke again the banter had gone from his voice. 'Were you in love with him?'

Coming out of the blue, the question took her by sur-prise. She found herself answering before she thought about it. 'I believed I was.'

'How long were you together?'

'Five months.' Jessica made an abrupt movement. 'I don't see…'

'Living together?' he persisted.

'Co-habiting it's called these days,' she said tautly. 'For what business it is of yours!'

For all the notice he took she may as well not have spoken. 'You discovered he was seeing someone on the side?'

'How like men are men!' she mocked. 'Yes, he was seeing someone on the side. Only he failed to keep her on the side. I came back early from a friend's hen night to find the two of them in bed together. A momentary aberration I suppose *you'd* call it.'

'Not in those circumstances. Was it necessary to ditch your job too?'

'I needed a clean break,' she said flatly, abandoning the satire. 'Leonie and I kept in touch after she moved to London. It was her suggestion that I take a holiday before starting to look for a job there myself.'

'As she thinks you're still on the island, we could spend a little more time here.'

Jessica shook her head vehemently. 'You do as you like, but there's no way I'm staying another night!'

'How would you propose leaving?' he asked.

'How would *you* like your grandfather to know the truth?' she countered.

'You wouldn't.'

He was right, of course, but she wasn't about to back down. 'Don't count on it!'

'You wouldn't,' he repeated on a softer note. 'You don't have it in you.'

Jessica jerked her head away as he ran the back of a finger down her cheek. 'Cut it out, will you!'

'That isn't what you want,' he said. 'You might think me an out-and-out louse, but it doesn't alter the way I make you feel. It was there the moment we came into contact the other night.'

'Lust, nothing else!' she derided.

'It's a pretty good basis.'

'For what?'

Broad shoulders lifted. 'Remains to be seen.'

'You'd do better to concentrate on how you're going to handle this supposed wedding,' Jessica returned hardily, fighting the undoubted temptation. 'There has to be a limit to how long you can make the ''arrangements'' last. Unless you're planning on a spurious ceremony too?'

'It crossed my mind,' he admitted.

'Anything to keep your cousin from gaining an advantage. I gather there might not be a lot of love lost between the two of you?'

Zac's jaw tautened a fraction. 'Let's just say we hold very different viewpoints.'

'With regard to business?'

'With regard to most things.'

The two top logs fell in, sending a burst of flame up the chimney. Jessica stirred herself as Zac rose with the obvious intention of adding another log from the pile stacked in an alcove to one side of the fireplace.

'Don't bother for me. I'm ready for bed. Alone,' she added with purpose.

'What else?' he returned mockingly. 'Sleep well, green eyes!'

The way she felt right now, it was unlikely, she acknowledged, making her way from the room. He'd been right earlier: she did ache. And it wasn't going to go away.

Yet another restless night left her feeling decidedly sluggish. A shower went some way towards reviving her, but the thought of several more hours in the Prescotts' company was no help.

The April sun was welcome after yesterday's rain, the view from the bedroom window over rolling Dorset countryside very different from the one she'd left in Majorca, though no less captivating. She could well understand why the Prescotts had chosen to spend their retirement in this part of the country.

It was probably doubtful though that Esther would stay on alone here after her husband had gone. The house was too big for two, much less one. Taking into account the fact that women usually lived a piece longer than men to start with, and her apparent good health at present, it was possible that she was facing a good many years without him. Not a happy prospect.

She gave Zac no opportunity to reply when Henry Prescott asked at breakfast how long they would be staying.

'I'm afraid I couldn't get any time off,' she said, deploring her newfound facility for spur-of-the-moment concoction. 'I have to be at work tomorrow. Of course, Zac doesn't have to leave too.'

'You could ring through and ask for another couple of days,' Zac suggested smoothly.

'The sooner you get back, the sooner you can start on the wedding arrangements,' said his grandfather. The gaze he rested on Jessica's face was deliberative. 'Will your parents want to be involved in the arrangements?'

More lies coming up, she thought unhappily, searching her mind for some adequate response.

'In the circumstances, I think it's going to be simpler all round if we handle it ourselves,' Zac put in.

'No Register Office,' Henry asserted. 'Brady was married in church, the right and proper way!'

Zac's face remained impassive. 'I understand church weddings have to be booked months in advance.'

The expression that flickered across the older eyes gave Jessica the impression that he'd actually forgotten the shortage of time for a moment or two, though he sounded quite steady when he answered.

'It seems the Register Office it might have to be, then.'

He left it at that, to Jessica's relief. She couldn't have taken very much more without blurting out the truth.

'This is going from bad to worse!' she berated when she managed to get Zac in his own for a few minutes. 'Your grandfather's no fool. If he isn't already suspicious, he's going to be before long!'

'He doesn't have long,' Zac reminded her. 'His heart could give out any minute.'

'And if by chance he continues to defy the odds?'

'Then I'll simply have to face the music. What time were you considering leaving?' he added with irony.

Jessica made a helpless gesture. 'I don't know. Two? Three?'

'Let's make it three. We should be in London by six-thirty—seven at the latest. Plenty of time to find you a hotel.' He reached out unexpectedly to smooth a stray curl of chestnut hair into place, his smile mocking her involuntary reaction. 'Then it's goodbye.'

'Yes.'

She could think of nothing else to say. In a few hours he would be gone from her life. She could tell herself she was glad of it, but it wouldn't be wholly true. Faultless he wasn't, unforgettable he might very well prove to be.

Henry was quiet over lunch, his thoughts obviously turned inward. It couldn't be easy to come to terms with the knowledge of impending death at any age, Jessica reflected. Personally, she would prefer to be left in ignorance.

Taking her leave of him later, she could hardly bring herself to look him in the eye. When he kissed her cheek, and thanked her for taking the time and trouble to make the trip, she felt like a traitor.

'This has been the worst experience of my life!' she said with feeling in the car.

'I'd have thought finding Paul in bed with another woman ran it pretty close?' Zac returned.

The anticipated stab failed to penetrate very deeply. She hadn't thought about Paul much at all this past couple of days. There had been far too many other things on her mind.

'That was different,' she declared. 'It's also history.'

'No chance then, of you going back to him?'

'None,' she said flatly. 'Why the interest anyway?'

Zac's shrug was brief.

His seeming indifference stung. Yet what else might she expect from him? Jessica asked herself. Despite what he'd said last night, her role had only ever been temporary.

As predicted, they were in London by six-thirty. Zac insisted on booking a room at the Savoy for two nights. They took their leave in the foyer. Jessica forced a level tone.

'I can't say it's been a pleasure, because it hasn't.'

The expression that sprang in the grey eyes was a warning in itself, but short of creating a scene, there was no escape. It took everything she had to stay unresponsive to a kiss that stirred every vital inner part of her.

Zac said nothing when he released her at last, but simply turned on his heel and headed for the main doors. She didn't wait to see him disappear through them.

CHAPTER FOUR

THE double room was luxurious, the bathroom big enough to hold a dance in. Under other circumstances, Jessica would have thoroughly enjoyed the experience of staying in one of the city's top hotels. As it was, it meant little.

Unpacking was no priority. Especially when she'd only be here a couple of days. Reluctant to venture downstairs to eat, she ordered a light meal from room service. Looking back while she waited for it to arrive, she regretted giving up her job in Gloucester. Seeing Paul and her replacement together had been humiliating, true, but she should have stuck it out.

The evening wore on. She ate the beautifully prepared prawn salad and watched a little television, although she couldn't have said just what she was watching. The hunger growing in her had nothing to do with food. It was Zac she craved for.

When the knock came on the door, she assumed it must be a valet or someone calling to see if there was anything else she needed. She went reluctantly to answer it, heart leaping into her throat on seeing who was standing there.

Zac didn't wait for an invitation, kicking the door shut behind him as he took hold of her. Jessica melted into the passionate embrace, returning fire for fire, all rational thought suspended. She leaned against him helplessly when he finally lifted his head.

'I couldn't do it,' he said roughly.

'Do what?' she managed.

'Let you go.' He put his lips to her temple where the hair clung. 'Not with so much to be resolved between us.'

Jessica made a supreme effort to bring her mind to bear on the words rather than the actions.

'Such as what exactly?' she whispered.

'The future,' he said. '*Our* future.'

'We don't have a future.'

'We could.' His tone softened. 'Marry me, Jessica.'

The shock of it struck her dumb for several moments. She gazed at him blankly.

'What game are you playing now?' she got out.

'I'm serious,' he said. 'I want you to marry me.'

Green eyes darkened. 'Just to make sure of a few shares?'

Zac shook his head. 'Not just the shares. Not just to satisfy grandfather either.'

'Oh, then it must be love, of course!' The sarcasm was a defence of sorts. 'Three days to fall head over heels!'

'The time is irrelevant,' he said. 'We belong together.'

'You can't say that!' Her voice had a crack in it. 'You know almost nothing about me!'

'I know all I need to know.' The determination was there in his eyes, in the set of his jaw. 'I won't give up on this, Jess. The way you responded just now, you can hardly claim to have no feelings at all for *me*.'

'There are feelings and feelings,' she said, battling her weaker instincts. 'What we have isn't love.'

Something flickered deep down in the greyness, but his tone didn't alter. 'It can be part of it. A very vital part.'

Jessica steeled herself as he put his lips to hers again, but there was no resisting the surging response, no shutting out the inner voice urging her to let matters take their own course. She found her fingers easing the suit jacket from his back, dropping it to the floor to seek the buttons of his shirt with an urgency echoed in his own dextrous movements.

Her nipples sprang to his touch as both blouse and bra

joined his garments on the floor, the ache increasing to almost unbearable proportions when Zac lowered his head to run the very tip of his tongue over the tender flesh. Her skirt slid all the way down her legs, leaving her nude but for the flimsy lace panties that were no barrier against the gentle caress.

She buried her face in the broad expanse of his chest as he swung her up in his arms to carry her across to the wide, canopied bed. Laid there, she watched through slitted eyes as he stood back to remove the rest of his clothing, stirred to even greater depths by the sleek muscularity of waist and hip, the masculine strength in the taut thighs. Already fully aroused, he was magnificent—the essence of manhood in all its prime. Jessica had never wanted anything as much as she wanted what was about to happen between them right now.

She reached for him eagerly, wantonly, as he lowered himself to her side, hearing his sharp intake of breath at the exquisite sensation. With Zac she felt no restriction, just an overpowering desire to explore every inch of the superb male body—to open herself to his exploration—to have him inside her, a part of her.

Zac kissed her again before removing the scrap of material that was the only hindrance left. His touch was delicate, parting the quivering flesh to find the warm, welcoming softness within—drawing a gasp from her own lips as he delved her secret depths. Back arching, face constricted, she gave herself up to the movement, the cry torn from her as she climaxed smothered as he claimed her lips once more.

'For you,' he said softly. 'Now this is for both of us.'

He played her like a violin, his lips and tongue wreaking havoc in their exploration of her whole body, making her writhe in an ecstasy of sensation. She wrapped her arms about the broad shoulders as they merged at last, lost to everything but the moment. They reached the summit in perfect unison, collapsing together to lie in suspended animation while the world steadied around them again.

It took the sudden chill when Zac lifted his weight from her to fetch Jessica back from the land of milk and honey. He didn't go far, propping himself on an elbow the way he had done that very first night, the smile on his lips echoed in his eyes as he viewed her.

'I owe you an apology,' he said. 'I'm afraid the practicalities went completely from mind. Not a habit of mine, I assure you.'

'If you're worried about me being pregnant, you don't need to be,' she murmured. She searched the hard-boned features uncertainly, trying, without success, to read the mind behind the grey eyes.

'What are you thinking?' he asked softly.

'That most people offered the same opportunity would probably grab it with both hands,' she admitted.

'It isn't an offer I'd consider making to most people.'

'Then why me in particular?'

Zac studied her arresting face, framed by the spread of chestnut curls over the pillow, dropping his gaze down the curvaceous length of her body and back again with another slow smile. 'I'd say the answer to that was pretty obvious.'

'I don't have anything a thousand other women don't have,' she insisted.

'I haven't had dealings with a thousand other women,' he returned equably. 'Anyway, there's a lot more to it than just looks. The spark was there from the word go. All it needed was the match.'

'I'd as soon do without the clichés,' she retorted, evoking a swift grin.

'There go some of my best lines!'

Looking into the laughing grey eyes, Jessica felt as if a hand had gripped her heart. It would be so easy to love this man. Why on earth was she hesitating?'

Easy to love, maybe, came the answer, but what about trust? Was it really her he wanted, or just a means to an end?

'Your grandfather...' she began, and saw the laughter fade, his mouth take on a straighter line.

'I can't pretend he isn't a factor, but only insofar as the time element is concerned.'

Jessica kept her tone level. 'You mean, you'd still want me to marry you if he died tonight?'

Zac returned her gaze without a flicker. 'I've never been against marriage itself. I just never met anyone I could contemplate being with on any permanent basis before.'

'Which you can with me?'

'Very much so.'

What was she waiting for? Jessica asked herself. How many times in her life was she going to be offered all that Zac could give her? There might be little real depth to what they felt for each other as yet, but that could be true of many a marriage in its early stages.

'All right,' she said recklessly. 'Let's do it!'

She closed her eyes as his mouth sought hers again.

Waking at first light to see a head on the pillow next to her, Jessica thought for a fleeting moment that she was back in the flat with Paul. Memory brought little reassurance. Last night had been sheer madness! How could she possibly contemplate marrying a man she barely knew?

Judging from his steady breathing, Zac was still deeply asleep. She slid slowly and carefully from the bed, and pulled on her cotton wrap, standing for a moment to gather herself.

The scattering of clothing across the floor bore mute testimony to just how wild a night it had been. She followed the trail, gathering the garments up as she went. A bare week ago she hadn't even known Zac Prescott existed!

It wasn't going to happen, of course. Zac would have second thoughts too in the cold light of day. What he needed to do this morning was go back to Dorset and clear things up. His grandfather might be angry enough to do as his grandmother had intimated, but that was a chance he would simply have to take.

As to herself, she would be doing as originally planned and taking advantage of Leonie's offer. If the idea held little appeal, that was something *she* was just going to have to live with.

She was standing at the window looking out at the river scene when the strong male arms encircled her waist.

'Why didn't you waken me?' Zac asked softly, nuzzling her ear. 'I know a far better stimulant than coffee!'

'Don't men ever think of *any*thing else?' Jessica jerked out.

'Depends on the place, the time and the incentive,' came the undaunted answer. 'Particularly the last. I can't have enough of you!'

Gritting her teeth, she put the coffee cup down on the sill. 'You've had all of me you're going to get.'

He gave a low laugh. 'That's fighting talk, lady!'

'I mean it!' She caught at the hand sliding between the edges of her wrap, knowing if he touched her the way he was aiming to do she'd be lost. 'Let go of me, Zac! I want you to let go of me!'

He did so immediately, standing back with hands raised in mock defence as she turned to face him. He was wearing one of the white towelling robes from the bathroom. It gaped at the chest, revealing the wiry thicket of dark hair she had found such a stimulant last night. She ran the tip of her tongue over lips gone dry, desisting abruptly on seeing the look in the grey eyes as they followed the movement.

Zac put his hands down and leaned against the nearby chest of drawers. His regard was devoid now of humour. 'So, why the change of mind?' he asked. 'You were all for it last night.'

'Not all.' Jessica did her best to at least sound in control. 'I let my better judgement be put aside for a time, but I knew deep down that it couldn't possibly work out.'

'Give me reasons why not,' he said levelly.

'Because it would be for all the *wrong* reasons. The only thing we have in common is sexual attraction.'

'Not true. Not from my side, at any rate. As I told you last night, there's a whole lot more to you than a face and body. I like being with you. I was under the impression that you felt much the same way about me.'

'It isn't enough,' she declared. 'You've no idea what love is.'

Zac studied her with a certain cynicism. 'Are you all that sure *you* do?'

About to return a short sharp affirmative, Jessica caught herself up. Did she though? If she'd truly loved Paul, would she have got over him as fast as she appeared to have done? Would she have even considered marrying another man within a few weeks?

'I know enough to be sure that what we have isn't anywhere near it,' she said at length.

'Maybe not yet. We can learn together.' Zac hadn't moved from his position, but there was nothing indolent about him. 'I'm not giving up on this, Jess!'

She looked back at him helplessly, rent by opposing forces. Dark hair tousled, jawline shadowed, the towelling

robe that was so obviously his only covering on the verge
of falling all the way open, he stirred every part of her.

Zac settled the conflict by reaching for her, drawing her
close to kiss her with a passion she couldn't hold out
against. She felt the swift sure touch of his hands at the
tie belt of her wrap, then the garment came loose, expos-
ing her to the exquisite sensation of skin to skin; tying
her innards in knots that could only be untangled one way.

'Come back to bed,' he murmured.

Whatever doubts she still harboured deep down, the
rapture to be found in Zac's arms was more than a match
for them. Lying utterly drained afterwards, she could only
compare what she felt like right now with what she'd
known in the past. With no other experience to draw on,
she had taken it that Paul's self-interest was typical of all
men. Zac had certainly rid her of *that* notion. Her pleasure
was so obviously as important to him as his own.

No more hesitation, she resolved. If this wasn't love, it
was certainly heading that way. They had the rest of their
lives to get to know one another.

Her objections to ordering breakfast for two via room
service were rendered invalid when Zac informed her that
he'd booked the room in the name of Mr and Mrs
Prescott.

'You were so sure of me?' she said.

'Sure I wasn't going to give you up without one hell
of a struggle,' he returned. 'I left you to save a scene in
the foyer, that's all.'

'Then created one kissing me the way you did,' she
accused.

'A mere parting gesture between husband and wife. A
little premature, perhaps, but good practice for the future.'

Jessica had to smile. 'I'll remind you of that the first
time you forget.'

'See me off the same way every morning, and there's no chance!'

There was something in that statement that bothered her a little, but the thought passed from mind as she contemplated the more immediate future. Mrs Zachary Prescott! Who would ever have believed it?

She opted for coffee and croissants from room service, watching in some bemusement as Zac demolished a full English breakfast.

'How do you manage to keep so fit if you eat like that every day?' she queried.

'I don't,' he said. 'Not every day. I just happen to have a need for extra sustenance this morning.' The grey eyes crinkled at the corners. 'Can't imagine why!'

'It's going to be difficult telling Leonie about us,' she said. 'She thinks I gave you the brush-off.'

'So, I refused to be brushed off.'

'But aren't you going to feel rather...awkward? I mean, considering the circumstances?'

Zac gave her a speculative glance. 'Anything that's taken place between Leonie and me happened before I knew you even existed. You must know her well enough to have a fair idea of her reaction. She'll be surprised, naturally, but she'll take it in her stride. She takes everything in her stride.'

Jessica could agree with that assessment up to a point. She'd yet to see her cousin thrown by events. Only this was surely a case on its own.

'Just how much *do* I tell her?' she queried.

Zac lifted his shoulders. 'I see no need to bring Grandfather into it.'

'Not even to explain why we're getting married in such a hurry?'

'We don't have to explain it,' he said. 'It's entirely our

own affair. We'll start the ball rolling this morning.' He paused. 'What about your parents?'

What about them? she almost asked, biting it back to say instead, 'I'll be contacting them, of course.'

Dark brows lifted. 'Contacting?'

Jessica met his gaze with an equability she was far from feeling. 'I haven't seen all that much of them since the divorce. They live opposite ends of the country now.'

'It's hardly that big a country.' Zac studied her thoughtfully. 'What kind of a relationship did you have with them before the divorce?'

'Not terribly close,' she admitted. 'They spent most of the time at loggerheads with each other.'

'With you in the middle.'

'On the periphery. I learned to stay out of it as much as possible.'

'Could be things might have been better all round if they'd divorced a great deal earlier than they did.'

'They probably would have done if it hadn't been for the hotel. Finally, even that failed to keep them together.'

The grey eyes held an empathic expression. 'It sounds as if you had a hellish childhood.'

'Not really,' she said. 'They were never hard, just a bit indifferent.' She hesitated. 'How's *your* mother going to react to all this?'

His smile was brief. 'She'll be happy enough once she's met you. She always wanted a daughter.'

A daughter-in-law was hardly the same thing, Jessica reflected. 'You must miss your father a great deal still,' she said.'

'Yes, I do. He'd have liked you,' he added. 'Grandfather does.'

'With some reservations,' she suggested lightly.

'True.' The smile this time was teasing. 'You're a mite

too lippy at times, he thinks, but that's up to me to do something about.'

'I'll make a note to be properly subservient the next time we see him.' Jessica sobered again at the thought of how little time he might have.

'How long is it since your cousin Brady got married?' she asked after a moment.

'Nearly a year.' Zac had sobered too. 'His wife is pregnant, hence the increased pressure on me to at least make a move toward following suit.' He paused, regard veiled. 'Were you serious about wanting children yourself?'

Jessica lifted her shoulders, hardly knowing which way to answer. 'It isn't something I've ever given any thought to. I just told your grandfather what I believed he'd want to hear.'

'Right.' There was no telling what his own thoughts on the subject might be. He put down his knife and fork and pushed back his chair. 'We'd better get moving.'

Jessica made the appropriate answer, only too happy to put the question from mind. She would need to be a whole lot more certain of the long-term future before she gave it any consideration at all.

The morning went by on wings. With time at a premium, Zac jumped at the offer of a slot fallen free at the Register Office on the following Monday due to a cancellation. From there they went on to Aspreys, where Jessica was invited to choose both engagement and wedding rings.

'I still can't believe it's only three days since we met!' she exclaimed over a late lunch. She lifted her left hand to look at the diamond hoop once more, seeing the stones flash as they caught the light. 'This must have cost the earth!'

Zac looked amused. 'The only woman I ever met with a concern for my pocket!'

'I've told you before,' she responded with mock sever-ity. 'You've been mixing with the wrong type!' She so-bered again to add, 'Speaking of which—'

'All in the past.' Zac was still smiling, but there was a note in his voice that hadn't been there before. 'As with your Paul, I hope.'

'He isn't *my* Paul,' she said. 'He probably never was.'

'You think he was two-timing you all the time you were together?'

'I suppose it's possible.' Jessica shook herself mentally, regretting the turn the conversation had taken. 'It isn't important anyway. Not any more. Did you make any de-cision about the Valldemosa hotel?'

Zac accepted the change of subject without demur. 'Not yet.'

'Do you often do that sort of thing?'

He gave her a quizzical look. 'You consider it beneath my lofty position to go out on the road?'

'I'd imagine it's pretty unusual.'

'It probably is. I'd go crazy sitting around an office all day and every day, so I take the chance whenever I can.'

'How much of the world does Orbis cover?'

'Just about anywhere people might want to go. The Maldives are getting to be one of the biggest draws.'

'Have you been there?'

'A couple of times. Wonderful scuba diving. Have you ever done any?'

Jessica shook her head. 'I've always wanted to handle a snorkel!'

'Easy enough to learn. Fancy it?'

She laughed. 'Some chance!'

'Every chance,' he corrected. 'There are tiny islands out there that are just made for honeymooners.'

It took Jessica a moment or two to come up with a response. 'I thought we'd already had the honeymoon.'

It was Zac's turn to laugh. 'I doubt if we'll be the first to have anticipated.' He lowered his voice to a seductive murmur. 'Imagine nights making love under a starry sky on a bed of pure white sand, with no need for clothing because there's no one else there to see us.'

Jessica could imagine it only too vividly. The very thought set the blood sizzling in her veins. 'Are you serious?' she questioned uncertainly. 'About going there, I mean?'

'Unless you know of somewhere even better?'

'From the sound of it, there can't be any!' She was too entranced for any blasé act. 'I've never been outside Europe before.'

'High time you did, then,' he said. 'There's a lot of world out there.'

Much of which he would already have seen himself, Jessica guessed. As a Prescott wife, she would be living on a different level from the one she was accustomed to.

'Of course, it's going to have to wait a while,' Zac added.

She took his meaning at once. He would hardly want to be out of the country with his grandfather in the state he was.

'Of course,' she echoed.

'I'm assuming you'll be going to Leonie's place tomorrow when you supposedly get back from Majorca,' he went on. 'Best if you give her the news on your own, I think. I'll come round on Wednesday. In the meantime, I'd better show you where you'll be living once we're married.'

Jessica's thoughts hadn't got that far ahead as yet. 'A flat?' she hazarded.

'A bit less conventional than that. You might not care for it.'

'I'm sure it will be perfect,' she said.

She had no reason to change that opinion when she saw the Chelsea mews. It was an absolute delight, every dwelling different, plant life abounding in every corner. Zac had both floors of number eleven. A dream of a place all round, Jessica acknowledged, roaming through the imaginatively decorated and furnished rooms.

'A designer friend's doing,' Zac admitted when she congratulated him on his taste. 'I wouldn't have known where to start.'

A woman, no doubt, she reflected. Possibly rather more than just a friend too. As a bachelor, Zac had enjoyed the freedom to spend his nights however he chose. There was every chance he was going to find the curtailment of that freedom hard to take.

'Hungry?' he asked.

Not for food, she could have told him. She shook her head.

'Coffee then? Or something stronger?'

'Coffee will be fine. Let me make it,' she tagged on as he made a move in the direction of the kitchen.

'I can manage,' he said. 'I even cook the odd meal.'

'I'll have to do something to earn my keep,' she responded flippantly.

Amusement gave way to some other, less easily defined emotion. 'You won't have to *earn* anything.'

He went from the room before she could come up with a reply, leaving her to the conclusion that she'd caught him on the raw with the unthinking remark. She found the idea reassuring in the sense that it suggested a certain vulnerability on his part: a way through, if she worked at it, to the inner man she needed to find if this marriage of theirs was to stand any chance at all of succeeding.

Whatever his feelings, he had them well under control by the time he brought the coffee in. Jessica eyed him over the rim of her cup as he took a seat on the far side of the three-seater sofa, the ache inside her increasing by the moment as she viewed the strong lines of his profile, the breadth of shoulder and muscular upper arm structure emphasised by the cream silk shirt he was wearing—the firm line of his thigh beneath the fine linen trousers.

Unable to stand it any longer, she put her cup down on the table in front of them, and reached to do the same with his, moving over to put both hands about his face and draw it down to reach his mouth with hers.

The sofa was more than big enough to accommodate them, the cushions supportive, the passion all-consuming. It was some time before either of them could gather the strength to move.

'That,' Zac murmured at last, 'was worth waiting for! Not that you did,' he added with a hint of humour. 'And there was I trying to be all considerate, thinking you'd be too tired!'

'I'll never be too tired for this,' she claimed huskily.

'Let's hope I can live up to demands, then.'

There was something in his voice that gave her pause for a moment, but she wasn't sure enough of herself to start probing for possible hidden meanings.

'As if,' she said, 'there could ever be any doubt about that!'

'As if,' he echoed drily. He planted a fleeting kiss on her lips, then eased himself upright. 'You'll find everything you need in the en suite. I'll take the guest room shower.'

Jessica had thought he might suggest they share a shower, the way they'd done that morning while waiting for room service, but the cabinets here weren't really big enough, she supposed, to hold two people.

The possibility that he'd had enough of her for one day, she refused to contemplate.

If she needed reassurance on that score, it was provided

back at the hotel, where they spent the night again. By morning, Jessica had reached a state not even the coming meeting with her cousin could demolish. If it wasn't love she and Zac shared, it was a wonderful substitute!

He left her at ten. Safe in the knowledge that Leonie would be at work all day, she took a taxi to the flat in St John's Wood, using the key and code already provided to let herself in.

Like the Majorcan apartment, the place was beautifully done out. At twenty-nine, Leonie was in a position to afford some of the best in life. Deservedly so too.

Jessica spent the afternoon on steadily increasing tenterhooks. Her cousin's homecoming at seven was small relief.

Blonde hair swept back in a smooth French pleat from her fine-boned face, slim, elegant figure clad in a designer suit in soft grey, Leonie looked delighted to see her.

'You should have let me know you were coming in today,' she chided. 'I might have been out for the evening. What time did you get here, anyway?'

'Around lunchtime.' Jessica hesitated, wondering whether to wait a while before breaking the news. Yet to what purpose? Now, or later, it had to be gone through.

'I have something to tell you,' she said. 'It's going to be quite a shock.'

'Really?' Leonie looked intrigued. 'What is it?'

Jessica drew a deep breath. 'I'm going to marry Zac Prescott.'

CHAPTER FIVE

LEONIE laughed. 'That certainly would be a shock! Do you have any other jokes stored up?'

Actions, Jessica decided, spoke louder than words. She held out her left hand, seeing astonishment leap in her cousin's eyes.

'I don't believe it!' Leonie exclaimed. 'You and *Zac*? It's only a few days since you said you'd blown him out of the water!'

Jessica fought the temptation to blurt out the whole story. 'I lied,' she said, thinking that much at least was the truth. 'I didn't know how to tell you.'

'Tell me what? That the two of you had fallen for each other on sight?'

'Something like that, I suppose.'

'Well, I'll be dammed! Zac Prescott, of all people!' Leonie shook her head, apparently more taken aback than upset by the news. 'Just goes to show the age of miracles isn't yet past!'

'You don't mind then?' Jessica ventured.

'Mind? Oh, you mean because I had him first?' She shook her head. 'I won't pretend I'll not miss our occasional encounters, but we were neither of us under any illusions. You've more reason to resent me, in fact.'

'I don't,' Jessica assured her, not entirely certain that that was the complete truth either. 'As Zac said, anything that happened between the two of you was before he met me.'

'Right enough. This is certainly going to be one in the

68

eye for Paul! Not that he obviously means a thing to you any more.'

'No.' Jessica could say that much with total honesty. 'I haven't even thought about him in days.'

'Hardly surprising. There's absolutely no comparison between what you had with him and what you'll have with Zac.'

'It isn't about material things!'

Leonie gave a sly grin. 'A secondary consideration, I'll grant you, but hardly to be sniffed at.'

'Did you never meet with Zac here in London?' Jessica asked after a moment.

'No. We preferred to stick to the occasional fling out there. What can't be altered must be endured,' Leonie added candidly. 'You're the one he asked to marry him. The *only* one, by all accounts.'

Claiming that she had no feelings whatsoever about their past relationship would not only be a waste of breath but a further bending of the truth too, Jessica admitted. Leonie was one on her own in that respect. One on her own in most respects, in fact.

Her cousin proved that by refraining from any in-depth probing over the evening, prepared, it seemed, to take the situation at face value. Asked her opinion of the island where she'd spent the past week, Jessica was glad to be able to return a totally truthful answer for once.

'I can understand why you bought there,' she concluded. 'It's the perfect place to switch off after a hard week.'

Relaxed on a sofa, Leonie inclined her head. 'Isn't it just. Nice to get away from everything on occasion—including men! Zac excluded, of course,' she tagged on blandly.

Jessica pulled a face at her, aware of being teased. The

thought still reckoned, but she could handle it. She was going to be handling a whole lot more.

Leonie was out of the room when the phone rang at nine. Jessica answered it, heart leaping when she heard Zac's voice. He wasted little time on greetings.

'There was a message on the answering machine when I got in this morning,' he said. 'Grandfather wants to have the wedding down there. He's already contacted the vicar. Apparently, it can be managed on Saturday.'

Head whirling, Jessica blurted out the first thing that came to mind. 'I thought you said it took months to organise a church wedding? What about banns and such?'

'With a common licence, and another from the bishop, it's possible to do without banns being read. I've got everything in hand.'

'But the time!' she protested. 'It simply can't be done!'

'No reason why not,' came the measured response. 'We can travel down on Friday. That gives you two clear days to do what you have to do. Time enough to contact your parents.'

Jessica made an effort to pull herself together. This week or next? What difference did it make?

'You've obviously no objections yourself,' she said.

'No,' he confirmed. 'We can take a few days somewhere along the coast afterwards.'

To be on hand should the need arise, Jessica assumed. Understandable in the circumstances, of course.

'Whatever you think,' she said restrainedly.

His laugh was a reassurance in itself. 'Practising subservience already?'

'One swallow doth not a summer make,' she responded.

'Now who's indulging in clichés?' There was a pause, a change of tone. 'How did Leonie take the news?'

The intimation that her cousin's reactions were of any

importance to him stirred an emotion becoming all too familiar.

'Why don't you ask her?' she said. She held out the phone to her cousin, who had just returned to the room. 'Zac would like a word.'

Leonie took the handset from her without comment. Her tone was easy as she addressed the man on the other end of the line. 'I believe congratulations are in order.'

She listened for a moment to what Zac had to say, her expression giving little way. 'Kismet, obviously. Well, sure. No reason at all. Saturday?' Her brows lifted a fraction, her eyes seeking Jessica's. 'Can't be done, I'm afraid. I'll be away on business. My very best wishes to you both, anyway.'

She handed the instrument back, returning to her reclining position on the sofa. Jessica hoped she sounded as natural as she took up the call again.

'So, when shall I see you?'

'I'll fetch you over here in the morning,' Zac said. 'You'll be more central for shopping. Long or short, make it white, will you? Grandfather's a traditionalist, as you might have gathered.'

'He's hardly likely to approve our cohabiting before the wedding then.'

'He doesn't have to know.' There was a slight edge to his voice. 'I take it you've no objection to premarital relations yourself?'

The irony stung. 'Obviously not,' she returned tartly.

His sigh was clearly audible. 'Sorry, that was uncalled for. We're both of us under pressure. I'll see you in the morning.'

He cut the call before she could respond. She replaced the receiver in its rest feeling decidedly downbeat.

'I get the feeling there's rather more to this than meets the eye,' Leonie observed. 'Want to talk about it?'

Jessica's hesitation was brief. Much as she needed to unload, she was too aware of how it would look. To marry in the throes of overpowering love was one thing, to do it for the reasons she and Zac were doing it was quite another. 'Hardly likely to last very long' would be the least of Leonie's comments.

'There's nothing to talk about,' she denied. 'If I seem a bit distracted, it's just that everything seems to be happening so fast! Zac's grandfather wants us to get married from his home down in Dorset.'

'So he said.' It was obvious that Leonie wasn't totally deceived. 'Nice of him to indulge the old man. Afraid I won't be able to make the wedding myself. I'm working in Frankfurt over the weekend.'

Jessica made the appropriate noises, scarcely knowing whether to be glad or sorry. There was every chance that it would finish up with just the four of them, anyway, because she very much doubted if either of her parents would attend. They both had their own very separate lives to lead.

Leonie made no further mention of Zac at all until she was leaving for work the following morning.

'I'm not doing any more prying,' she said. 'I just hope you know what you're doing.'

'I do.' Jessica wished she could convince herself of it. 'Everything is absolutely fine!'

The doubts didn't wholly disappear on sight of Zac shortly afterwards, but they became immaterial in his embrace. When he kissed her like this, with every evidence of having missed her as much as she had missed him last night, she could think of nothing else.

The morning traffic was heavy. It took them almost an hour to make it to Chelsea. Jessica's spirits were dampened again when Zac departed almost immediately for the office, although she could understand his need to be there after several days away, and more to come. In the meantime, she was hardly short of things to do.

She began by unpacking. She'd brought nothing but her clothes and a few personal items away from the rented flat she had shared with Paul, so her whole life was contained in the two suitcases.

There was a wall of wardrobes in the master bedroom. She fingered through the suits and casual clothing already stored there, visualising the well-honed male body they were made for. Tonight they would share a bed again. Every night from now on, in fact. She knew a sudden swelling resolve. They were going to make a go of this. They couldn't fail to make a go of it!

The unpacking completed, she considered her options. It was midday already, but she still had the afternoon and the whole of tomorrow to do what she had to do. White, Zac had said, so white it would be. Anything to make his grandfather happy in his declining days.

One thing she certainly didn't need to do was set about any housework. Zac hadn't mentioned any domestic help, but he must employ someone to keep everything so pristine. She had no quarrel with that. The thought of spending her days dusting and polishing held little appeal. Although willing to indulge Henry Prescott's ideals up to a point, she had no intention of remaining a stay-at-home wife either. Zac could surely find her a job with the company.

She had just finished a light lunch when the domestic help arrived. The woman who let herself into the house with a key was in her mid-thirties; her tailored overall bore a logo Jessica recognised as that of a well known agency. From the newcomer's lack of surprise on seeing her, she deduced that this wasn't the first time overnight visitors had been found lingering.

'Sorry to disturb you,' the woman proffered with more than a hint of irony. 'I'm here to do the cleaning.'

Jessica gave a smile. 'I'm Jessica Saunders. Mr Prescott's fiancée.'

That did gain a reaction. 'Fiancée!'

'That's right.' Jessica kept the smile going. 'And you are?'

'Barbara Manners. I've been cleaning for Zac for the last twelve months.'

Jessica wasn't slow to note the slight emphasis on her use of Zac's first name. Typical of him not to stand on ceremony, though she wouldn't have thought the two of them met up very often if this was the hour Barbara usually arrived.

'Well, just do what you normally do,' she said lamely.

She took herself to task as the other went on through to the kitchen. So Barbara was an attractive woman, not all that much older than Zac himself. Was she going to suspect him of bedding every attractive female he came into contact with?

Somehow reluctant to leave her alone in the house, she rescheduled the shopping trip for the following day, and took it on herself to sort out laundry from the basket in the main bedroom, although there wasn't a great deal. The small utility off the kitchen held a combined washer-dryer. Barbara came into the room as she loaded it.

'I always do that on a Friday,' she said. 'The ironing too. Zac's very particular about his shirts.'

Jessica said mildly, 'I'll leave you to it in future, then. I was going to make coffee. Would you like a cup?'

She made the coffee, and took it through on a tray to the sitting room where Barbara was running a quite unnecessary vacuum over the carpet.

'Sit down for a few minutes,' she invited.

The other woman perched on the arm of a chair, her gaze speculative as she took the cup Jessica handed her.

'It's a bit of a shock, I must say,' she remarked. 'I had Zac down as a sworn bachelor! Known him long, have you?'

Jessica kept her tone light. 'Long enough.'

'Well, I can't blame you for snapping him up. Not that I envy you the job you're going to have. I know what it's like being married to a man used to variety. Vows don't mean a great deal when the sap rises.'

'There are exceptions to every rule,' Jessica returned, determined not to let the cynicism get to her.

Barbara gave a short laugh. 'So they say.' She drained the cup, and got back to her feet. 'Must get on. I've another job to go to after this.'

She left at three, having first stacked the dried laundry in a basket ready for Friday. Knowing it was sheer perversity on her part, Jessica set up the ironing board and spent the next half hour on a job that had never held any great appeal for her at the best of times. What she did like to do was cook on occasion, but the refrigerator held little to inspire her. Zac, she guessed, would more often than not eat out.

That particular problem was solved when Zac rang to say Leonie had contacted him to invite the two of them over for dinner that evening.

'She'd have phoned you,' he said, 'only she didn't have the number. I'm ex-directory,' he added, anticipating the question that leapt to Jessica's mind. 'Anyway, I'll make sure I'm home early enough to make it back across town for eight.'

She could hardly keep the two of them apart indefinitely, Jessica acknowledged, struggling to overcome her reluctance to see them together. She would just have to put a rein on her imagination.

Zac got in at six-thirty, surprised to see the freshly ironed shirts Jessica had hung to air on the wardrobe door before putting them away.

'There was no need for this,' he said mildly. 'Barbara does the laundry on a Friday. I completely forgot to tell you about her. Must have had other things on my mind,' he added with a smile that slowly changed character as he viewed her appearance in the silky black trousers and pale cream top. 'Speaking of which—'

'We don't have time,' Jessica interjected with reluctance. 'You still have to shower and change.'

His shrug made light of the moment. 'I guess it will keep.'

He exchanged the suit in which he'd spent the day for a pair of cord trousers and a designer T-shirt, shrugging on a beige suede jacket that sat on his frame the way only bespoke tailoring could. Looking at him, Jessica still found it difficult to consider it was only a matter of days since they'd first met. Most couples getting married had at least been together long enough to have some understanding. Apart from the obvious, they knew so little of one another.

With traffic at its heaviest, it was gone eight by the time they made it to St John's Wood. Neither Leonie nor Zac showed any awkwardness in their greeting. Jessica did her best to act naturally herself. Leonie had invited a friend to make up a foursome. Around the same age as Zac, he proved to be very good company. He was something big in information technology from what Jessica could gather.

'Any chance of a lasting relationship?' she asked her cousin when they had a few minutes on their own in the kitchen.

'With Greg?' Leonie laughed, shaking her head. 'He'd

run a mile if I showed any sign of getting serious! Same here.'

'Do you plan on staying single all your life?' Jessica said curiously.

'Depends on whether I ever meet a man I could contemplate spending my life with. You already cornered the best of the bunch.' She turned a glance when Jessica failed to answer, her smile brief. 'Just teasing again. You should know me by now. Anyway, how's it going so far?'

Jessica made an effort to infuse enthusiasm. 'Fine! He has a mews cottage in Chelsea. It's absolutely gorgeous!'

'Not quite what I'd have imagined him to choose,' Leonie commented. 'Though I can see the advantages. Getting the car off the road, for one.' She paused, her regard too shrewd for comfort. 'I don't see you going in for domesticity wholesale.'

'I've no intention,' Jessica acknowledged. 'I'll be looking for a job.'

'With Prescotts?'

'Hopefully.'

'You've discussed it with Zac?'

'Not yet.' Jessica slanted a glance. 'You doubt he'll agree?'

Leonie gave a brief shrug. 'Who am I to say what he will or won't do?'

'You've known him longer than I have. And you're very much alike in outlook.'

'Depends on the direction. I certainly never saw him as a hook, line and sinker man. But then, who can ever know? You've proved a regular bundle of surprises yourself. After your experience with Paul, this is the last thing I'd have expected of you. Meeting to marriage in one short week! You have to admit, there's a distinct ring of fairy tale in there.'

Jessica forced a smile, a lighter note. 'With a happy ending!'

'I hope so. For both your sakes.'

There was no more said on the subject, to Jessica's relief. It was only too obvious that her cousin was far from convinced of the reasons for this marriage.

'Leonie's suspicious,' she said on the way back to Chelsea.

'Of what?' Zac asked.

'The time element, for one thing. She seems to find it difficult to believe that you of all people could fall that far that fast.'

'So it's just *my* feelings she doubts?' he said after a moment.

'Mine too, considering I was supposed to be still getting over Paul.'

'She thinks you were caught on the rebound?'

'Something like that.'

'Then we'll just have to convince her she's wrong on both counts.'

Jessica gave him a swift glance, but there was no reading anything from the profile etched against the sodium street lighting. What was she looking for anyway? she asked herself. She already knew exactly where she stood in his estimation: the same place he stood in hers. Whether there would ever be more was a question only time could answer.

The drive down to Dorset on Friday was accomplished in sunshine, with a forecast for a fine weekend to come; a welcome change from the damp and dismal days just passed.

Jessica viewed the coming events with mixed feelings. While Henry Prescott's condition appeared to have remained static over the past week, his impending death was bound to cast a shadow over the whole proceedings. It was only to be hoped he'd at least see the ceremony through.

Which was more than her parents were going to do. They'd both of them expressed themselves delighted for her, but each found pressing reasons why they couldn't possibly attend the wedding. Something of a relief, Jessica had to admit. The two of them together would hardly have enhanced the weekend. She could just imagine Henry Prescott's reaction to their constant wrangling.

Zac's mother had returned to her family in Scotland on his father's death. Jessica had spoken to her on the phone, and found her pleasant enough on the surface, though there had been more than a hint of underlying doubt concerning the marriage itself. Hardly surprising, considering the suddenness of it. She would be travelling down today too by train.

As Zac hadn't mentioned anyone else, it seemed safe to assume it would be just the five of them at church. With no one of her own attending, Jessica was glad about that. Less stressful for Henry Prescott too.

'Do you think your grandmother was being quite truthful last night when she said your grandfather was just the same?' she ventured.

'Probably not,' Zac admitted. 'She sounded evasive. No reason to let the blues take over though. He wouldn't appreciate it.'

Recalling the old man's attitude, Jessica could only agree. The way to treat him was as though nothing at all was wrong.

They reached the house just after six. Esther came out to greet them, her manner subdued.

'Your mother's been delayed. She'll be coming down overnight,' she said. 'But Brady and Sarah will be here for dinner. I'm sorry your parents weren't able to make it,' she added to Jessica.

Jessica murmured something appropriate, aware that as Zac had expressed no surprise over the news that his cousin and wife were expected, he must have known they were coming. He could at least have warned her!

Henry Prescott looked no different physically from when they had last seen him. He greeted the two of them benevolently.

'You'll be wanting to get yourselves settled,' he said. 'We can talk later.'

They were to occupy the same rooms as before. Jessica confronted Zac in his.

'Why didn't you tell me the whole family was going to be here?' she demanded.

'It didn't occur to me,' he returned mildly. 'What's the problem, anyway? You had to meet them sometime.'

He had a point, Jessica had to admit. And she probably should have anticipated it. She spread her hands in a rueful gesture. 'I know that. It's just…'

'Just that you've no one of your own coming,' he finished for her as she paused. 'Those parents of yours should be ashamed of themselves. Your mother, at least, might have stirred herself!'

Jessica kept her tone matter-of-fact. 'She had something else already arranged. Anyway, it isn't really that. More the thought of facing your family *en masse*.'

'Five people hardly constitute a mass. Anyway, you'll cope. You handled Grandfather pretty well.' He put out a hand, his smile an invitation. 'Come here a minute.'

She went willingly, meeting the kiss with an ardour she couldn't withhold. Zac ran his hands down her back to bring her up closer against him, his arousal as instant as hers. He made a rueful gesture of his own when he reluctantly let her go.

'Not the time, and definitely not the place, I'm afraid.'
Grey eyes looked deep into green, expression soft. 'You
never fail me.'

'Tell me that after next weekend,' she answered huskily.

They went downstairs again after changing for the evening, to find the others already arrived. Zac performed
introductions with easy assurance. With only a few
months between them, the cousins were close enough in
looks to be taken for brothers. It was only around the
mouth that they differed to any degree. Brady's lacked
any sign of humour in its set.

Blonde and pretty, Sarah Prescott was quite a bit
younger than Jessica had somehow anticipated. No more
than twenty-two, she guessed. Judging from the bulge
swelling her slender form, the pregnancy was already well
advanced.

'You're certainly not wasting any time!' remarked
Brady with what Jessica considered a dire lack of sensi-
tivity in his grandfather's hearing. 'I understand the two
of you have only known one another a few weeks?'

'That's right,' Zac confirmed. 'I saw and was con-
quered! The best thing that ever happened to me!'

'We're not married yet,' Jessica quipped, responding to
the hint of tongue-in-cheek. 'I may turn out to be a real
termagant once I have that ring on my finger!'

'Up to Zac to put you in your place if you do,' declared
the patriarch of the family. 'No Prescott worthy of the
name allows his womenfolk to rule the roost!'

Not about to cause him any upset, Jessica adopted a
meeker tone. 'I'll certainly bear that in mind.'

Sarah made a sound suspiciously like a giggle, turning
it into a cough as Brady looked her way with a frown.
'Bit of a tickle,' she claimed.

Not quite the mild little thing she'd appeared to be on

first sight, Jessica suspected, catching the hint of laughter in the blue eyes.

The lack of rapport between the cousins became more than evident as the evening progressed. Apart from the physical similarities, they had little in common. If Henry noted the discord, he paid it no attention. He seemed distracted, Jessica thought, glancing his way from time to time. She hoped it wasn't a sign of strain.

By tacit consent, they none of them lingered beyond his hour of retirement at ten.

'Thank goodness that's over!' Jessica exclaimed softly on the way upstairs.

'There's my mother to meet, and the wedding to get through before we're done,' Zac rejoined.

'You make it sound like a trial!' she said with an attempt at humour.

Zac laughed. 'With a life sentence at the end of it!'

'Hardly compulsory in this day and age.'

They had reached her bedroom door. He paused, looking at her with quizzical expression. 'You don't see the marriage lasting?'

Jessica kept her tone light. 'Who can ever tell?' She pressed a kiss to his lips before he could form an answer, and left him standing there.

Inside the room with the door closed against him, she stood for a moment to collect her thoughts. So Zac saw the wedding as something to be got through: a lot of men probably felt the same about the actual ceremony. The difference being the reason for having the ceremony at all. Without some depth of emotion behind it, from both sides, what *real* chance was there of the marriage lasting?

There was a little comfort in retiring to bed alone after the past two nights of unrestricted love-making. No way was Zac going to risk upsetting his grandmother by coming to her room, of course, but she hoped he was suffering the same degree of frustration.

It wasn't just the sex she was missing though, she acknowledged. She'd grown used to his being there when she woke in the night: to feeling the weight of his arm about her waist, hearing his steady breathing. Paul had never held her like that, even at the start. If she were honest with herself, the disillusionment had begun long before she found him in bed with Sally that night.

If she were honest with herself, came the rider, she would also admit that her feelings for Zac already went a piece deeper than she tried making out. Deeper than his for her at present, almost certainly. At least as his wife she would be batting from an inside position, so to speak.

CHAPTER SIX

WITH the wedding set for three in the afternoon, it wasn't deemed necessary to bring breakfast forward from its usual nine o'clock slot. It was supposedly bad luck for the bridegroom to see the bride prior to the ceremony on the day, Jessica recalled, but there wasn't really much choice when they were both staying in the same place.

The patriarch of the family appeared to be fully recovered from whatever it was that had kept him so quiet last night. He had a self-satisfied air about him, as if he and he alone had brought the occasion about.

Which he had in a way, Jessica conceded. If his condition hadn't impelled Zac to desperation straits, they'd have probably gone their separate ways.

Isabel Prescott arrived at ten. In her mid fifties and comfortably built, her bobbed dark hair frankly greying, she was far from the image Jessica had formed in her mind's eye. She liked her instantly.

'Sorry for the change of plan,' Isabel apologised. 'Blue had her puppies the night before last. A whole week early! I had to make sure she was going to be all right before I left them with my brother and his wife. Blue's my German Shepherd,' she tagged on for Jessica's benefit.

'You'd have done better to have her spayed,' said Brady.

'And deny her the chance to be a mother even once?' came the mild reply.

'How many?' Jessica asked impulsively. 'Puppies, I mean?'

The older woman's eyes warmed. 'Four. One of them all white. Can't imagine how that happened!'

'Are you quite sure the Samoyed next door didn't get to her before you took her to the stud dog?' asked Zac on a humorous note, and received a twinkle in response.

'Could be possible, I suppose.'

'You'll not be able to sell any of them as pure breds if there's any doubt about it,' said Brady.

'I wouldn't be *selling* them anyway,' she answered with a touch of asperity. 'They're going to friends who'll love them whatever their pedigree.'

Good for her! Jessica silently applauded as Brady turned away with a meaningful shrug. Money wasn't everything to everyone!

She had no opportunity to be alone with Zac throughout the morning. Henry monopolised both grandsons. To Jessica, he appeared to enjoy playing the two of them off against one another—an uncharitable thought she did her best to put aside. Having met Brady, she could better appreciate Zac's view of him. Given the power, he would sweep all before him.

She ate little at lunch. At two, she went up to shower and put on the sleeveless silk sheath that lightly skimmed her body down to the ankles. The pearl strand and studs Zac had bought her as a wedding present, plus a simple silver bracelet she already owned, were to be her only jewellery.

Missing companionship, she felt her spirits lift when Sarah popped her head round the bedroom door to ask if she would like a little help.

'You could put my hair up for me,' she said. 'It takes ages to do it on my own.'

'Glad to,' the younger girl agreed. 'Have a seat.'

Jessica did so, viewing the other through the mirror as

she piled the chestnut thickness into a knot of curls with enviable dexterity.

'Gorgeous hair,' Sarah commented. 'Gorgeous altogether, in fact. Zac's a lucky man!'

'I'm the lucky one,' Jessica answered lightly.

'Oh, I'll agree there too. I could fancy him myself!' She gave a gamine grin. 'Not that I'd want Brady to hear me say that. You might have gathered they're not all that close.'

'They certainly look alike,' Jessica commented.

The expression that crossed Sarah's face was come and gone too quickly for analysis. 'Quite different in character though,' she said.

Taking up the spray of lilies of the valley, she attached it with a couple of hairpins across the front of the topknot, standing back to view the result with a satisfied nod. 'Perfect! You'll knock 'em all dead!'

A rather unfortunate way of putting it, considering the circumstances, Jessica thought, but if Sarah was aware of any gaffe, she didn't show it.

'I'd better get off,' she declared. 'Zac and Brady are going ahead, so I'm to drive Aunt Isabel and Grandmama to the church.' She bent impulsively and pressed a swift kiss to Jessica's cheek. 'Glad to have you on board!'

The gesture warmed Jessica's heart, making her feel not quite so alone. In Sarah, she sensed a friend.

Henry had elected, in the absence of her father, to give her away. He was waiting for her when she came downstairs, the others having already left for the church. He nodded approval of her appearance.

'Very nice, my dear. A credit to the family!'

'Are you going to be all right?' Jessica asked anxiously, searching the thin features.

Just for a moment he seemed to hesitate, an odd expression in his eyes, then he shook his head as if in dismissal of some thought. 'I'll be perfectly all right. That sounds like the car arriving. Shall we go.'

It took them only ten minutes to the little village church. Jessica was surprised, and somewhat disconcerted, to find many locals occupying the pews. Tall, dark and devastating in a charcoal suit, Zac gave her an encouraging smile as she joined him before the altar.

'You look wonderful!' he murmured.

The service went by in a flash. Signing her maiden name in the registry for the last time, Jessica allowed herself no regrets. She was starting a new life. One she intended making the very best she could of.

Sarah came to press another kiss to her cheek as they emerged into sunshine again, her pretty face aglow. 'All the happiness in the world!' she said. 'You too, of course, Zac.'

Her husband echoed the sentiments, if with rather less ebullience. Jessica doubted if there would be many family get-togethers once this was over. She wondered what had drawn a girl of Sarah's vivacity to a man like Brady, who so seldom let go with a smile, much less a laugh.

It took her mother-in-law to make her feel really at home. 'I'm glad Zac waited till now,' was all she said, but it was enough.

Dulcie had prepared a quite superb buffet back at the house. There was Champagne too, although Zac drank no more than sufficed for the toasts. His grandfather showed no such forbearance. Watching him toss back his third glass, Jessica took it that he'd decided to live his life to the full in his final days. All the same, she was surprised that no one made any attempt to stop him.

'The old man always did like a tipple,' said Brady, misreading her expression. 'He can hold it.'

'I suppose it doesn't really matter any more,' Jessica returned wryly.

Dark brows drew together. 'Meaning what?'

His tone flustered her. 'Well, it isn't going to make much difference to the outcome, is it?' she said uncertainly. 'If I only had a short time to live, I'd probably do the same.'

'A short time to live?' Brady's frown deepened. 'What gave you that idea? Apart from a touch of angina, he's as strong as an ox!'

He hadn't been told, thought Jessica in dismay. Why on earth hadn't Esther warned her? She wondered if she and Zac were the only ones who did know—and if so, why?

She looked back to the man in his chair by the window, fighting a creeping suspicion as she studied him. He had never looked like a man all that close to death. Supposing, just supposing, it was all a fabrication: a ruse to force Zac not only into proving that the girl he'd ostensibly fallen for really existed, but to marrying her into the bargain. Zac had said himself that he could be ruthless.

It couldn't be true! she told herself. Surely no man would consider putting his own flesh and blood through such an ordeal just to get his own way? Surely no wife would consent to go along with it?

Esther was looking her way when she glanced across. The plea in the older eyes was all the verification needed. Jessica found her voice with an effort.

'I must have misunderstood.'

Brady viewed her with cynicism. 'So it seems. Is Zac labouring under the same misunderstanding?'

'I'm...not sure.'

'Oh, I think you are,' he said. 'It explains all this. He thought there was a chance of the old man cutting him off if he didn't show willing in the marital stakes.' He smiled sourly. 'I'll give him top marks for effort! Pity it was for nothing.'

Jessica's eyes blazed sudden green fire. 'This might have happened a bit sooner than it would have done, but it certainly isn't for nothing!'

'Not for you, maybe. Although I wouldn't count on holding his interest for too long. A regular Don Juan, is Zac. He's had more women than I've had hot dinners!'

He was getting a real kick out of this, Jessica realised. A wholly malicious one too. What she wasn't about to do was give him the satisfaction of seeing her true feelings at this moment.

'Understandable,' she said. '*He's* every woman's dream of a man!'

The point went home, bringing a nasty glint to the grey eyes. 'Only till they wake up.'

Isabel appeared at Jessica's elbow as she opened her mouth to deliver another broadside. Her mother-in-law looked from her to Brady with some speculation.

'Your wife went to lie down,' she said. 'I think she's just tired, but perhaps you should go and make sure. Her time can't be all that far off.'

'It's another eight weeks yet,' Brady responded, making no move.

Isabel held her gaze. 'All the same…'

He took the hint, albeit with reluctance. Isabel turned her attention to Jessica with a smile. 'Men can be so dense at times, don't you find?'

Jessica found a smile of her own, if a strained one. 'Not up to now.'

'Oh, I'm not talking about Zac. He's always been quick on the uptake.'

Not this time, Jessica reflected hollowly. If he'd realised what his grandparents were up to, she wouldn't be standing here now.

'Are *you* all right?' asked Isabel on a concerned note. 'You've lost colour.'

Jessica shook herself mentally. 'Too much Champagne, I expect. It never did suit me very much.'

'Me neither. I never could see what all the fuss was about. Personally, I'd as soon have a glass of apple juice.' She paused, her expression softening as she surveyed the striking face beneath the crown of lilies. 'Zac's a very lucky man to have found you, Jessica. I have to confess, I was a bit concerned about the short time you've known one another, but I can see there's nothing to worry about. I've asked him to bring you up to Scotland as soon as possible to meet my family. You will come, won't you?'

There was only one answer Jessica could make. 'Of course. I'll look forward to it.' She felt her lips go stiff again as she caught Zac's signal from across the room. 'I'd better go and change,' she added.

'Oh, yes, you're going down the coast for a few days. I'd have thought Zac might find the time to take you somewhere a little more romantic, but I don't suppose it really matters where you spend your honeymoon.'

From the sound of it, Jessica could only conclude that Zac hadn't seen fit to pass on the news of his grandfather's alleged condition to his mother either. But then, he'd hardly want her to see the marriage as nothing more than a means to an end? Which was all it really was, of course. To do him credit, he'd never tried to make out that love played any real part in the relationship.

Upstairs in the bedroom, she took off the silk dress and sat down at the dressing mirror in her filmy underwear to renew her make-up. The face gazing back at her looked normal enough, green eyes surprisingly steady. Zac had to know the truth, of course. The realisation that he'd been tricked into this hasty marriage was hardly scheduled to enhance the honeymoon, but she could hardly keep it from him.

She was still sitting there when the door opened to ad-

mit the tall, grey-clad figure. Zac came over to slide both
hands over her bare shoulders, pressing a kiss to her nape.

'You look so utterly delicious!' he said softly. 'Good
enough to eat!'

Jessica steeled herself as he moved his hands down to
the clip of her bra. 'Not here,' she protested.

He laughed and desisted. 'You're right. We've the
whole night ahead of us. I'll go and get into something a
bit less formal. The place we're staying is very casual.
No dressing for dinner. No dressing at all, if we don't feel
like it,' he tagged on with the wicked sparkle she had
always found such a turn on.

Tell him now, Jessica urged herself as he moved back
to the door, but the words wouldn't come. There was
every possibility that he would storm downstairs to demand a reckoning. Better to leave it until later when they
were alone.

Wearing a lightweight suit in pale green, she went
downstairs to find Zac ready and waiting with their bags.
Isabel took leave of her with a kiss.

'Hope to see you again soon,' she said.

Looking tired still, Sarah gave her a hug, laughing over
the barrier caused by her 'bump'. They must get together,
the four of them, she declared. Meeting her husband's
eyes over her shoulder, Jessica read a very definite dis-
sension. She doubted, anyway, that Zac would want it.

She was quiet in the car. Zac turned a quizzical glance
after a few miles.

'Lost your voice, have you?'

'It's been a long day,' she said.

'It isn't over yet,' he returned. 'I missed you last night,
Jess. This morning too.'

Jessica felt her heart lurch. Would it really hurt, she
asked herself, to leave the telling until after the honeymoon? These coming few days with no outside distrac-

tions could make all the difference to their relationship. By the time she did tell him, it might not even matter any more.

'Same here,' she said.

His smile held a promise. 'We've plenty of time to make up for it.'

They began doing just that within fifteen minutes of reaching the small but exclusive hotel where Zac had booked the one and only suite. Anticipating an explosive reunion, Jessica was infinitely stirred by the unaccustomed tenderness in his love-making. It gave her hope of a deepening emotion on his part: deep enough, if she worked at it, for the news of his grandfather's plot to have lost its impact by the time he learned of it.

They certainly seemed to grow closer during the following days. The hotel was set in five acres of grounds, with miles of countryside beyond that to wander in. The sea was only a half a mile away. Zac went for a swim one morning, scorning Jessica's view that it was far too chilly at this time of year for more than a paddle.

'It's bracing,' he declared. 'Invigorating!'

'*I* don't need invigorating,' Jessica replied blandly, bringing a glint to the grey eyes.

She jumped back as he dropped the towel he was using to rub himself down and reached for her, but she was too late. The beads of cold water still adorning his body soaked through her shirt as he pulled her close, his mouth an irresistible force.

'I'm soaked!' she complained when he let her go.

'Teach you not to underestimate me,' he said.

Laughter bubbled on her lips. 'As if I'd ever do that.'

There was an answering smile on his lips as he surveyed her. 'Good thing you brought a jacket.'

Glancing down at herself, Jessica could see what he

meant. With no bra beneath the clinging T-shirt, there was little left to the imagination.

'I feel like a Page Three exhibit!' she claimed ruefully.

'There's a hell of a sight more erotica about the way you look right now than in any bare boob display,' Zac declared.

It was certainly having a visible effect on him, she noted as he turned away to continue drying himself. Stirring him physically was no problem. She only wished she could be as sure of his inner emotions.

He hadn't mentioned his grandfather all week. Nor had he called the house to ask how he was doing. Jessica had begun to wonder if he might have guessed the truth himself. If he had, it obviously didn't bother him too much, which gave her added hope.

That particular bubble burst on the Friday evening at dinner, when he expressed relief over the lack of communication.

'Grandmother has the number here,' he said. 'She'd have called if anything had happened. We'll go back and spend the weekend with them, anyway. It could be the last time we see him.'

Jessica swallowed on the dryness in her throat. Having kept it to herself the whole week made it no easier.

'There's something you should know,' she said huskily. 'Your grandfather isn't dying. Not in the near future, at any rate.'

The candlelight was reflected in the eyes boring into hers across the width of the table. 'What are you talking about?'

'It was all a pretence. A ruse to force you into proving yourself.'

Zac viewed her for several moments in silence, face blanked of expression. 'How do you know?' he asked at length.

'I mentioned it to Brady.'

'Brady!' The word was explosive.

'He said apart from a touch of angina, your grandfather is strong as an ox,' she carried on. 'Something of an over-statement, perhaps, but you have to admit he doesn't re-ally give the impression of a man on the brink of death.'

The grey eyes narrowed. 'You're saying you suspected he was lying from the first?'

Jessica shook her head. 'I just thought he was being very courageous about it. I know you said he could be ruthless, but it didn't occur to me that anyone could be *that* ruthless.'

'So why wait till now to tell me?'

It was the question she'd been dreading. She lifted her shoulders, fiddling with the stem of her wine glass. 'I wasn't sure how to tell you.'

'So you let me go on thinking there could be a phone call anytime.'

She forced herself to look at him, heart sinking as she met the chilly gaze. 'I'm sorry. It just seemed...' She broke off, spreading her hands in a helpless little gesture. 'It was too late anyway. The wedding was over.'

'It's never too late,' came the brusque response. 'If you want out—'

'I don't!' It was a cry from the heart. 'Can't,' she amended swiftly, afraid of having given too much away. 'If we break up, there's a good chance your grandfather will cut you from his will. We were neither of us under any illusion about this marriage to start with, so nothing's really changed?'

There was a lengthy pause before Zac responded. It was impossible to tell what thoughts were going through his mind. When he did speak it was with control.

'You're willing to carry on the way things are?'

'Yes,' she said. 'We can make it work, Zac.'

His lips slanted. 'In one department, at least. Could be a lot worse, I suppose.'

Jessica kept her voice steady with an effort. 'A whole lot worse. I realise you'll probably want to confront your grandfather at some point, but there's no reason for him to know there's anything contrived about our relationship.'

'You seem to have it all worked out,' Zac commented. 'Not that I'm complaining. Whatever it takes to keep the old devil sweet!' He took the wine bottle and refilled her glass, lifting his own in ironic salute. 'To a long and happy future!'

Jessica echoed the sentiment with heavy heart. Sex apart, the only thing keeping this marriage afloat was his fear of losing those damned shares! While ever his grandfather lived, he was stuck with the situation.

They made love as usual that night, but there was something definitely missing. Jessica lay sleepless for a long time afterwards, regretting ever having met Zac. He wasn't going to fall in love with her. Eventually, he would even stop wanting her. When that happened, she was out of it regardless.

They drove back to Whitegates the following morning. Esther's greeting was subdued.

'I'm really sorry for deceiving you,' she said to Zac, obviously taking it for granted that he'd been told the truth. 'You seemed so reluctant to bring Jessica to meet us, he began to doubt she existed. You know your grandfather. Once he gets an idea in his head there's no letting go.'

'And he bullied you into going along with it.' Zac smiled and shook his head as she opened her mouth to protest, bending to kiss her cheek. 'Don't worry about it.'

His grandmother might feel a lot less guilty if she knew

how right her husband had been, Jessica reflected, but Zac obviously had no intention of telling her. Henry Prescott didn't hold the monopoly on ruthlessness in this family—in the male line, at any rate.

They confronted the old man in the small sitting room, where he was ostensibly perusing a newspaper. There was no hint of contrition in the eyes he raised to the pair of them.

'So Brady let the cat out of the bag.'

Zac's jaw tautened. 'You mean he was in on it too?'

'Not until he asked me what was going on after Jessica here informed him I was dying.' The last with a faint smile. 'Not a total lie. We're all of us heading for death from the moment we're born.'

'Supposing Zac had mentioned it to Brady when he first heard?' asked Jessica.

'There was little chance of that. You must have realised for yourself that my grandsons converse only where absolutely necessary.' His gaze sharpened a fraction. 'Would it have made any difference if you'd known the truth?'

'Only in the time element,' Zac cut in before she could answer. 'We'd probably have waited a few more weeks, that's all.'

'No great harm done then. To the good, in fact. You've some catching up to do.'

Jessica took his meaning immediately. She opened her mouth to refute the suggestion, closing it again as she caught Zac's glance.

'What will be will be,' he said mildly. To his grandmother, hovering in the background, he added, 'Which room will we be using?'

'The one Brady and Sarah usually have,' she said, both sounding and looking relieved to have it over with. 'I'm so glad you're staying the night again.'

'Might be the last chance we get for a while,' Zac returned.

Esther's face lit up. 'I thought we'd have a barbecue this afternoon. Jimmy's cleaning up the grid and laying the charcoal now. Our odd-job man,' she added for Jessica's benefit. 'He can turn his hand to anything. Don't know how we'd manage without him!'

'We'd find somebody else,' said her husband complacently. 'Lunch in half an hour, you two, so don't go getting involved in anything up there.'

Jessica gave a weak smile. The way she felt at the moment, it was most unlikely.

The room they were to share was spacious, with a four-poster bed that would normally have delighted her. Her wedding dress was hung on the wardrobe front in mute reminder.

'You could at least have given him a piece of your mind for putting you through what he did!' she said with force. 'There's no wonder he thinks he's a law unto himself when you all kowtow to him the way you do!'

Zac shrugged. 'What point would there be? The deed's done. As we agreed last night, things could be a whole lot worse.'

As if to prove it, he drew her to him and kissed her, rousing her the way he always did.

'You heard what your grandfather said,' she murmured unsteadily against his lips. 'Lunch in half an hour. Twenty minutes now, in fact.'

'Time enough for some,' came the reply, 'but I was never into quickies.' He put her from him again, his smile cursory. 'It will save. Just unpack what you'll need for tonight. We'll be leaving right after breakfast.'

Jessica did so, wishing they could be on their way right now. The more she saw of Henry Prescott, the harder it was going to be to stop herself from telling him just what she thought of his underhand tactics. It was high time somebody did!

She went through the day with tongue held firmly in check—as much for Esther's sake as Zac's. *Her* marriage had taken place in an era when the man was still regarded as totalitarian head of the house. She'd probably never gone against him, and would no doubt find it upsetting if some other woman did.

The barbecue was some relief. Jessica and Zac shared the cooking, helped along by glasses of wine, while the older couple reclined on loungers on the wide patio.

Sheltered from the wind, it was wonderfully warm, the views superb. If things had been different, Jessica could have enjoyed spending further weekends down here. As it was, if they did come again it would be purely for show.

They left after lunch on the Sunday. Relieved though she was to be free of the constant temptation to tell Henry Prescott what she thought of his tactics, Jessica viewed their return to the mews cottage without enthusiasm. Zac would be going in to the office tomorrow, leaving her to do…what? She could get rid of Barbara and tackle the housework herself, but that was hardly going to tax her resources. She wasn't cut out to be a stay-at-home wife.

'I'm going to start looking for a job,' she stated after several miles had gone by. 'I'd go crazy cooped up in the house all day!'

'It's hardly a prison,' Zac returned drily. 'You've the whole city on the doorstep! An open cheque-book too, if that's what's bothering you.'

'I don't want your money!' Her tone was abrupt. 'I'd rather earn my own.'

'You know Grandfather's views on working wives,' he said after a moment.

Jessica gave him a stinging sideways glance. 'I realise

you'd do just about anything to stay in his good books, but there's a limit to how far *I'm* prepared to go. If you're worried about his reaction, he doesn't have to know.'

'You mean lie about it.'

'Only by omission.'

'That's splitting hairs.'

'It's maintaining the illusion,' she retaliated. 'The one you created to keep him sweet.'

A muscle jerked suddenly along the firm jawline. 'I didn't notice you putting up all that much resistance to the idea.'

She kept a cool tone with difficulty. 'I don't suppose I'm the first to allow principle to be overcome by lust. You're a hard man to resist, Zac.'

'Sure.' His mouth had twisted. 'Lucky we still have that much to keep us going. Assuming you weren't putting on an act last night, that is?'

Jessica rode the hurt. 'You know I wasn't.'

'I don't *know* anything,' he said. 'Women have a distinct advantage when it comes to sex. They don't have to prove arousal physically.'

'Why on earth would I bother pretending to enjoy it if I didn't?' she demanded. 'Like you said, it's the one thing we have. As long as it lasts, at any rate.'

Zac kept his gaze on the road ahead, his expression impassive. 'You see an end in sight?'

Swallowing on the lump in her throat, Jessica gave a brief shrug. 'Not yet, but you know what they say about the first flush.'

'Then we'd better make the most of it,' he said.

There was no further mention of the job business, but Jessica had no intention of giving up on it. Obviously, Zac wasn't going to find her anything, so she would fend for herself.

CHAPTER SEVEN

IT DIDN'T prove easy. Well thought of though she'd been in her previous job, her qualifications and experience fell somewhat short of requirements in London it seemed. After being accustomed to working for one man, the thought of general clerking held little appeal. The alternative was to find something completely different.

A part-time position advertised at a Kensington food store was too good an opportunity to miss. Working ten till four, five days a week, there was no need for Zac to know anything about it.

Jessica started on checkout, finding the work repetitive but not unendurable, the other staff friendly. The salary was no big deal, but it at least gave her some sense of independence.

Zac accepted her excuse that she'd been out shopping without question when he mentioned trying to get in touch a couple of times. He didn't say why he'd wanted to speak to her, and Jessica hesitated to ask. Relations between them were strained enough as it was. Largely due to her, she had to admit. No matter how hard she tried, she couldn't come to terms with the fact that she wouldn't be here at all in normal circumstances.

She did her best to appear properly grateful when he presented her with a mobile for use in emergencies, making a mental note to get rid of the one she'd had for years and rarely bothered with. It would have to be switched off when she was at work, of course, so she could only hope he wouldn't have cause to try contacting her during those hours.

The only place the barriers dropped completely was in bed. When Zac made love to her, nothing else existed. His unflagging desire was the one thing that kept her going. It couldn't last, of course. Not to the same degree. One of these nights he would plead tiredness after a long day, and the end would have begun.

Only too well aware of what Leonie's opinion would be, she made no mention of the job to her either, making out, when asked, that she was content to hang fire for a while on the matter. Her cousin was pretty busy with her own concerns, as it happened, leaving little opportunity for getting together. She brought Greg with her the one time she came to dinner at the mews, though still denying any serious involvement.

'I'm just not cut out for marriage,' she said in the kitchen where the two of them were making coffee while the men talked. 'Maybe I'll change my mind when I'm old and lonely, but in the meantime I'm happy the way I am—beholden to nobody.

'It certainly suits you though,' she added with a smiling glance. 'The look of a woman fully and frequently satisfied. Not that I'd expect any less of Zac, of course.'

Jessica let the comment pass, knowing there was no malice in the teasing. She still found it difficult to think about Leonie and Zac together in any intimate sense, but there was no point in getting upset about it. She was the one he made love to these days. The only one—or she'd better be!

The weekend they spent in Edinburgh with Isabel proved a great deal more enjoyable than she anticipated. The family consisted of a brother and wife, along with two married children who both lived within a few miles of the city with families of their own. Asked when they might consider taking the step themselves, Zac took it on himself to answer for them both with a smile and a shrug, giving the impression that they were already trying.

'I'm not having a baby just to please your grandfather!' Jessica stated when they were alone.

'I'm not asking you to,' Zac returned levelly. 'If we started a family, it would be because we both of us wanted it.'

Unlikely, then, Jessica reflected, stifling the pang. Children belonged in a proper, balanced relationship based on love and commitment, not an arrangement like theirs that could end any time.

'Sarah must be getting close now,' she said. 'Brady would have let you know, wouldn't he?'

'You can bet on it.' Zac's tone was dry. 'He insisted on knowing the sex as soon as it was possible. If it had proved to be a girl, he'd have gone up in flames! Sons are de rigueur in his eyes.'

Looking at him through the dressing table mirror as he slid cuff links into place, Jessica felt the usual stirring in the pit of her stomach, the wave of heat building swiftly from that central core. From the top of his well-groomed dark head to the tip of his hand-made shoes, he was pure masculinity. She wanted him desperately—any way she could have him, and for as long as she could have him.

Sensing her regard, he looked round, meeting her eyes through the mirror with a familiar glint springing in his own.

'You're insatiable!' he said softly. 'Not that I'm complaining. What man would?'

He came over and drew her to her feet, bending his head to kiss his way up the taut line of her throat to finally reach her lips. Jessica kissed him back with passion. She came down to earth with reluctance when he put her regretfully from him.

'We'll get back to this later. We're due at the restaurant in twenty minutes. Don't go cold on me.'

Some chance, she thought wryly. All he had to do was touch her to have the blood throbbing in her veins again.

They'd flown up on the Friday night. They travelled back Sunday evening, arriving home around midnight.

Zac was normally out of the house by eight-thirty at the latest. This particular Monday it was coming up to half-past nine when he finally departed, leaving Jessica to throw her things together and dash for the bus she knew had no chance of getting her to work on time.

She was twenty minutes late, and earned herself a severe ticking off from the self-important manager. Jessica controlled the urge to tell him what he could do with the job. Finding another offering the same advantages when it came to hours and proximity would be difficult, and she still couldn't face the thought of spending her days mooning around the house. In any case, she would miss the friends she'd already made here.

'Sour-faced old prune!' sympathised one of the latter who'd been in the vicinity, as Jessica took her place at the next checkout desk. 'Bet his wife gave him the elbow last night. Not that I'd blame her. He's a real misery guts!'

'I *was* late,' Jessica returned ruefully. 'I suppose he had reason to get a bit shirty.'

'A bit!' The other snorted. 'Doesn't know the meaning of moderation, that one!'

Jessica turned her attention to the young woman who'd just unloaded her trolley onto the belt, saying a cheery 'Hello' to the toddler in the folding seat. A boy around two years old, he returned her gaze with solemn intensity.

'He's been chattering away all round the shop,' declared his mother in fond exasperation. 'Now you'd think he didn't have a tongue in his head!'

Jessica smiled. 'He's quite right not to talk to strangers. What's his name?'

'Gavin,' she supplied. 'Just three, and a total pickle! I'm beginning to wish I hadn't been quite so emphatic about not having a nanny when he was born.'

'It isn't too late,' Jessica ventured, drawing a laugh and a shake of the head.

'Too much of a climb down. My husband would never let me forget it! He'll be going to nursery school before too long, anyway. That will at least give me a morning or two to myself.'

She went on chatting amiably while her goods were totalled, departing with a smile and a wave. Jessica could see part of the store car park from where she sat. The personalised number plate on the Range Rover into which the woman loaded both shopping and child was a status symbol in itself. In the nanny bracket financially, if not by choice, she judged.

She was late getting home that afternoon, because the manager insisted on her making up the time she'd lost. She got in bare minutes before Zac, who had elected to take early leave himself for once.

'Board meetings run me ragged!' he declared, pouring himself a stiff whisky. 'I'm seriously considering turning beachcomber on a desert island somewhere!' He viewed her over the rim of the glass, taking in her wind-blown hair and casual dress. 'What have you been doing with yourself?'

'I went to the Gardens,' Jessica lied. 'I felt like a walk. I took a taxi,' she added, anticipating the next question. 'There *and* back.'

The strong mouth took on a slant. 'I'd hardly expect you to go by bus. Maybe we should think about getting you a car of your own.'

'I'm not up to inner city driving,' she said. 'Anyway, there isn't room for another car in the mews.'

Zac studied her in silence for a moment, gaze too penetrating for comfort. 'We could move.'

'Where?' she asked.

'Out of the city. Richmond, perhaps. Somewhere less congested, at any rate.'

Somewhere better to raise a child, came the fleeting thought, followed by an emphatic shake of the head. 'I don't want to move. I like it here, within easy reach of everything.'

His shrug was easy. 'Fair enough. I can't say I'm all that eager to abandon the place myself. We're invited out to dinner tomorrow night, by the way. Ian Grant, one my fellow directors. His wife is about your age.'

'Just us?' Jessica asked.

'No, there'll be others there. Nothing too formal. That silver grey number you wore the other night will do fine.'

'I may not have moved in your circles before, but I don't need advising on how to dress,' she said shortly.

'That wasn't the intention.' Zac sounded short himself. 'Stop being so damned touchy!'

Jessica caught herself up before the snappy rejoinder could leave her lips. 'Sorry,' she proffered instead, trying to look it. 'I'm just feeling a bit on edge.'

He considered her pensively. 'About what?'

'Nothing. Everything.' She shook her head again, forcing a smile. 'It takes a lot of getting used to, this marriage lark. You must feel the same way yourself.'

'To a degree,' he admitted. 'But I'm not complaining. You're worth coming home to.'

She melted immediately. Zac was making every effort; the least she could do was reciprocate.

They made love on the sitting room floor, pillowed by cushions purloined from the sofas. Jessica only realised he wasn't using anything when it was too late to do anything about it. Not that she really wanted to, she had to admit. Making love in the raw, so to speak, was even more ravishing. She was still on the Pill, anyway.

She made sure to be on time at work the next morning, taking it that with a dinner engagement to get ready for, Zac might be early again. She needn't have worried as it happened, because it was almost seven o'clock when he arrived.

'Traffic,' he said succinctly. 'We'll be taking a taxi to the Grants'. It's parking by permit only in their area. You look good,' he added. 'I'll try to live up to you.'

The day he looked anything but good himself would be a first, Jessica reflected as he disappeared upstairs. She took a look at herself in a mirror, all prettied up in silver grey. An attractive enough sight, she supposed, though nothing particularly outstanding in her view. Leonie, for instance, could beat her for looks any day of the week!

The Grants, it turned out, lived in Kensington. Already on edge over the coming evening, Jessica felt her heart plunge even further as she registered the number plate on the Range Rover standing outside the elegant terraced home. She thought wildly of pleading a sudden migraine, but it was hardly going to be believed. All she could hope for was a lack of recognition on her hostess's part.

A hope doomed to failure from the moment of meeting. Cathy Grant placed her immediately.

'We already met,' she said as Zac performed introductions. 'Yesterday at the store.' The confusion was apparent in both eyes and voice. 'Have you worked there long?'

Jessica felt rather than saw Zac's reaction. Her gaze was fixed firmly on Cathy's face, her smile stiff as a board. 'A couple of weeks. How's Gavin?'

'Oh, fine! He's staying with his grandparents tonight.'

Cathy was making an obvious effort to put the questions that had to be crowding her mind aside. 'Ian will introduce you round,' she added. 'I just need to check the oven.'

Her husband led them through to a spacious drawing room where two other couples were already ensconced with drinks. Jessica acknowledged introductions without taking in a single name, aware of Zac's inwardly seething presence at her side. He was too well bred to make a scene in public, of course, but there was going to be hell to pay once he got her alone.

Perhaps sensing the atmosphere between them, Cathy made no further reference to their previous meeting, although the glances she occasionally cast from one to the other reflected her continuing bafflement. Jessica could appreciate her dilemma. Why would the wife of one of the company's major shareholders find it necessary to take a job in a retail food outlet? If she mentioned it to her husband—and she was almost sure to—then it would no doubt reach Brady's ears before long. That would really set Zac's blood on fire!

The evening seemed to go on for ever. Jessica yearned for it to end, yet dreaded what was surely to come. Zac held his tongue in the taxi going home, waiting until they were indoors with the doors closed against the outside world before letting fly.

'What the hell was all that about working in a supermarket?' he demanded.

'It isn't a supermarket,' Jessica answered, trying to keep a level head. 'It's a rather exclusive emporium catering to the needs of the upwardly mobile classes.'

Zac drew a harsh breath. 'Don't try making a joke of this! How do you think it reflects on me to have a wife serving on in a shop?'

Green eyes acquired a spark of their own. 'There's

nothing demeaning in it,' she retorted, giving up any idea of pacification. 'I'm not into that kind of snobbery!'

'You can call it what you like. The fact remains that you're doing a job you're not only over-qualified for, but have no need of to start with!' Zac was furiously, unnervingly angry, his whole face rigid. 'Why, for God's sake? You have your own account, your own cheque book. What on earth could you need the kind of pin money you must be earning at that place for?'

'It isn't the money,' she said. 'It's to do with self-respect. I refuse to live off you entirely.' She paused, hardening her mind against any retreat. 'You'll just have to accept it.'

It seemed impossible for his jaw to tauten any further, but it did. 'There's no way I'm going to accept it! You don't go near the place again, do you hear me?'

'I could scarcely fail to hear you,' she returned with asperity. 'And you can whistle! If you don't like the idea of my working in a shop, find me something you *would* consider acceptable. As you once said, you have the contacts.'

'I won't do that!'

'Because you're afraid of losing your grandfather's respect if he discovers you're incapable of keeping your wife in her proper place?' she lashed out. 'You're no different from Brady when it all boils down. What you'd really like is for me to get pregnant to put you back on par. Well, abandoning the condoms isn't going to do it, so you may as well forget it! I wouldn't bring a baby into this travesty of a marriage for a pension!'

Jessica broke off, aware of having gone a great deal further than ever intended. Zac was looking at her as if he'd never really seen her before. 'Travesty?' he said softly.

'Well, isn't it?' she defended. 'You married me to satisfy a self-centred old man who believes he has a God-given right to dictate the way others should live, no other reason. Your grandmother may have been brainwashed into following his every wish, but I refuse to go on paying court to his antediluvian ideas! I'm no docile little house-wife, Zac. I have a mind and a brain of my own!'

'I never had any doubt of it,' he returned. 'You knew what you were taking on when you agreed to marry me. Most people would consider you'd made a rather good deal on the whole.' He shook his head as she made to speak, his face set, his eyes like steel. 'If it isn't enough for you, I'll find you a job, but you don't go back to this store. Right?'

'I have to,' Jessica protested. 'I'll need to give notice.'

'So let them sue. I know someone in PR who's in need of a new secretary. I'll give him a ring first thing in the morning and tell him the good news.'

'How do you know he'll find me suitable?' she asked on a somewhat deflated note.

'He owes me a couple of favours,' came the crushing reply. 'Anyway, I'd say you were capable enough.'

Jessica stood in silence as he turned away. She'd made her point, she'd even won her point, so why didn't she feel any sense of satisfaction with the outcome?

The answer lay in Zac's demeanour towards her, so changed from the easy manner he usually employed. Not just the fact that she'd gone behind his back to take the job, but the very real probability that Brady would get to hear of it and lose no time in passing on the news to his grandfather. If Henry Prescott ran true to form, it could well result in a changed will. He was certainly capable of it.

For the first time, Zac made no attempt to touch her in any way when they were in bed. He lay on his side facing away from her, an acre of space between them. Jessica fought the urge to tell him she'd changed her mind about having a job. It would be living yet another lie. And for what? There was more to life than the feel of a man's arms about her.

The interview in Holbourn a few days later proved no more than a formality. Whatever Leo Brent's true impression of her capabilities, he showed no hesitation in offering her the job. She would be taking over from his present secretary who was leaving at short notice. He didn't say why the other woman was going, and Jessica didn't ask. Zac would hardly have put her in line for the job if there'd been anything untoward about the man.

Having heard nothing from the shop, she could only assume that Zac had handled that matter too. She should have held out for a right and proper notice period, she knew, but she had to confess to a secret relief that she hadn't had to fabricate reasons for leaving after such a short time.

The bedtime stand-off had lasted no more than the one night. Jessica was sorely tempted to tell him to get lost when he drew her into his arms as usual the following night, but with her pulses already galloping, she lacked the strength of mind to carry it through.

Sex might not be the answer to everything, but it certainly helped, she told herself cynically as she composed herself for sleep afterwards. Zac obviously thought so too.

She spent a day learning the ropes from the retiring secretary. The other was to accompany her husband to America where his company was transferring him.

'I didn't want to go at first,' she confessed over lunch. 'I like the life we have here. Patrick would have turned the job down if I'd insisted, but I couldn't do that to him. Anyway, it's only for three years.' She laughed. 'Ten to one I'll not want to come back when the time comes!'

'Murphy's law.' Jessica smiled back. She waited a moment or two before saying casually, 'What's Mr Brent like to work for?'

'Leo,' the other corrected. 'He'll insist you call him that. He's a nice guy. Divorced four years, but a real pussy-cat of a boss. It was a relief to him when your husband put you up for the job. Meant he didn't have to carry out any more interviews.' Her glance was curious. 'I shouldn't have thought you'd have need of a job, married to a Prescott.'

'A whim on my part,' Jessica told her smilingly.

'A lasting one, I hope,' came the candid reply. 'Leo deserves a little devotion.'

She moved on to other matters after that, leaving Jessica with the impression that there might have been more than one reason for her reluctance to move to America.

It took her less than a week of working for Leo Brent to appreciate her predecessor's feelings. No more than medium height and looks, with an unruly thatch of fair hair that made him appear younger than his forty-two years, he exuded the kind of benevolent charm most women would find a draw.

He'd met Zac a couple of years before when working on publicity for the Orbis take-over Zac himself had gone out on a limb to promote.

'Turned out a winner,' he said with some personal satisfaction. 'A smack in the eye for that cousin of his who voted against it. Of the two of them, Zac has by far the better business sense. It's to be hoped he's the one to take the chair when it comes up for grabs next year.'

Which wouldn't be likely if Brady inherited all their grandfather's holdings, Jessica reflected. Henry Prescott's death may no longer be imminent, but the pressure still existed. It could quite easily be another ten years or more before the man breathed his last. A lifetime, if he continued to hold the same threat over his grandsons' heads.

If word of her stint in the retail world had reached Brady's ears, Zac made no mention of it. He made no reference to the job she was doing either. The atmosphere between them was like sitting on a volcano, waiting for something to erupt. When he made love to her it was with passion, but precious little tenderness. Hardly surprising, she supposed, when their whole relationship was based on the former rather than the latter.

'I'm not sure how long I can stick this for!' she burst out one night after waiting in vain for some sign of emotional involvement on his part—*any* sign. 'I feel like a whore!'

'Whores rarely experience orgasm,' came the seemingly unmoved response. 'If that was acting just now, you made the wrong career move!'

There was a pause, a sudden heavy sigh. He drew her back to him, his kiss soft on her lips. 'You're right. I've been a boor. How about we agree to differ over the job thing, and start over?'

Jessica didn't hesitate. Compromise was better by far than warfare. She gave her answer in deed rather than word, rousing him to life again—though this time in far gentler mode.

There was hope for this marriage of theirs yet, she thought in the hazy, lazy aftermath of their love-making, when they lay entwined in each other's arms. They were closer at this moment in every sense than they had ever been.

CHAPTER EIGHT

SARAH'S totally unexpected call the following week co-incided with Zac's overnight trip to France on company business.

'I thought it time the two of us got to know each other a little better,' she said: 'How about lunch tomorrow to start with? I know this little place in Covent Garden that does an absolutely glorious *boeuf en croute*!' She laughed. 'Food becomes all-important when you're feeding two!'

'I can imagine,' Jessica sympathised. She hesitated. 'You must be getting close now.'

'Oh, there's another couple of weeks yet,' came the airy reply. 'Probably more. First babies are more often late than early. The men don't have to know about it. Not yet, anyway. We can spring it on them later when we're firm friends. It's about time they stopped feuding themselves.'

Jessica could only agree, though she doubted it happening. She had an hour and a half lunch break, and Covent Garden was easily reached from the office, so there was nothing to stop her from taking up the suggestion.

'Okay, fine,' she said.

They arranged to meet at twelve-thirty. Replacing the receiver, Jessica contemplated telling Zac about it if he rang later. However he might feel about Brady, he'd been friendly enough towards Sarah. He could surely have no objection to their seeing one another.

The question was resolved by his failure to make the call. Retiring to bed alone that night for the first time in weeks, she lay wondering what he was doing right now.

Subsidiary companies were apt to lay on entertainment for visiting VIPs. For all she knew, he was out on the town with some French woman detailed to give him a good time.

She was being paranoid, and she knew it, but it made little difference. What it all boiled down to was that she still didn't really trust him when it came to other women.

Sarah was at the restaurant before her. She looked radiant, hair and skin blooming with health and vitality.

'I expected to feel thoroughly done in by now after carrying Junior around for eight and a half months,' she declared cheerily when Jessica complimented her on her appearance, 'but I never felt better! Not that I shan't be happy to have a waistline again. Maternity clothes leave a lot to be desired in the way of fashion.'

She eyed Jessica with undisguised speculation. 'You look a bit drained yourself. You wouldn't, by any chance, be pregnant too?'

'Not by any chance,' Jessica denied smilingly.

The speculation increased. 'You and Zac don't want children?'

'Not just yet, at any rate.'

'That's not going to put you in favour with Grandfather Henry.'

Jessica viewed the pretty face across the table in some uncertainty. 'That's surely not the only reason you and Brady decided to start a family?'

'Oh, no. We'd no intention of waiting. Brady knew when he married me how much I wanted children. I always did. Ever since I had my first doll.' She gave the sparkly little laugh again. 'I can hardly wait to see the little love in the flesh! Scans don't give all that good a picture. We already named him. Richard Henry Prescott.' She wrinkled her nose. 'I'm none too keen on the Henry myself, but Brady insisted. The initials aren't bad at least. RHP—Right Honourable Person. Useful if he becomes Prime Minister.'

'Very,' Jessica agreed. She hesitated before saying diffidently, 'Do you always give way to Brady's preferences?'

'Most times,' came the untroubled answer. 'He tends to take after his grandfather in many ways, and I'm not one for rocking any boats unnecessarily. Men like to think they're in charge. Gives their egos a boost. I don't imagine Zac's any different.'

Jessica contented herself with a smile and a shrug by way of a reply, not about to be drawn. Zac was strongminded, true, but far from egotistical.

The food proved to be as good as Sarah had forecast. It was only gradually that Jessica realised the younger girl was simply picking at her plate. The animation had faded, the faint line drawn between her brows an indication of some inner conflict.

'What is it?' Jessica asked urgently, seeing the line deepen even as she looked.

The blue eyes lifted to hers were surprisingly serene. 'I think I may have started,' she said. 'I've just had a second contraction, about fifteen minutes since the first. Stronger this time too. It might be a good idea if I get out of here before my waters break. It might put the other diners off their meal.'

Jessica lost no time in calling for the bill. She also got the desk to order a taxi. Sarah was booked into a private hospital. By the time they reached the place, the pains were coming every seven minutes.

'Will you call Brady?' Sarah requested before she was wheeled away. She handed over her bag. 'You'll find his mobile number in the front of my diary if he's not at the office. Tell him to get here as soon as possible,' she added, face compressing again as another contraction started. 'He wants to see the birth.'

The way things were going, it was likely that he was going to miss it, Jessica thought, but she could but try.

She got through to Prescotts on her own mobile, to be told Brady was still out to lunch. While it was likely that his set would be switched off while he was at table, she called the number she had found in the diary, vastly relieved when he answered.

Thankfully, he wasted no time on questions that could be answered later. He was on the other side of town, it appeared, which meant he would have to contend with the midday traffic. Considering what Sarah had said earlier, Jessica wouldn't have been all that surprised if he'd commanded her to tell his wife to hold the baby back until he got there.

Having done all she could in that direction, she went to see how matters were proceeding. Sarah was already in the delivery room, she was told on reaching the floor. In the absence of a husband to hold the patient's hand, she was asked if she would like to put on a gown and do the honours herself.

Sarah greeted her appearance with tearful gratitude. 'It's all happening so fast!' she said between contractions almost running together. 'Brady is going to be so disappointed! You'll have to tell him every detail, Jessica.'

If she judged correctly, a second-hand account of his son's first appearance in the world would be the last thing he'd want, Jessica reflected wryly, giving her assurance.

She'd once seen a birth on television, but the real-life experience was infinitely more moving. The hand Sarah was clinging to felt gripped by a vice in those final moments as the baby's head emerged, yet she was too involved in what was happening to be really conscious of any pain.

There were satisfied smiles and exclamations from the attendant staff when Richard Henry Prescott let out a hearty bawl as he was lifted clear.

'Nothing wrong with this one's lungs!' declared the midwife. 'A good eight pounds, if I'm not mistaken!'

She proved right within a quarter of a pound. Wrapped in a light blanket, the child was brought back to Sarah, who was now propped up in bed looking amazingly fresh after her ordeal.

'Isn't he beautiful?' she exclaimed, searching the small, perfectly formed features. 'He looks just like his daddy!'

He did, Jessica was bound to admit. He even sported a shock of dark hair. Like all new born babies, his eyes were blue at present, but they'd no doubt turn grey later. The Prescott genes were not easily overcome.

Looking from child to mother, she felt a stirring of something close to envy. Sarah had no doubts about her marriage. She held the proof of it in her arms.

She stayed with her until Brady arrived, leaving the two of them alone to share their little miracle. Her mobile rang as she made her way down to the reception area. Zac sounded abrupt.

'Leo says you didn't come back from lunch. Where the devil are you? It's gone half-past three!'

'I'm at the hospital,' Jessica responded. 'Sarah had her baby sooner than expected. I should have called Leo to explain, but it all happened so fast it completely went from mind. Where are you, anyway?'

'At home,' he said. 'I got an earlier flight.' The pause was brief. 'How come you were involved?'

'Sarah and I were having lunch together when she started. Unfortunately, Brady missed it all, but he's there with her now. A boy,' she added. 'Eight pounds, four ounces. Both doing well.'

'Glad to hear it.' Zac paused again. 'How long have you and Sarah been meeting up?'

'This was the first time. She rang me last night to suggest it.'

'Any idea why?'

Jessica began a shrug, desisting on the realisation that he couldn't very well see her. 'I don't think there was any particular reason. She just thought it time we met up again. A good thing, as it happened. We were a lot closer to the hospital than she would have been at home. I'd better ring Leo and let him know what's happening. I'll see you later.'

She rang off before he could say anything further, her eyes on the calendar pinned to a notice board opposite where she stood. Today was Wednesday. She and Zac had been married six weeks the previous Saturday. She'd had one period a week or so after the wedding, which meant she had been due again the previous week.

Looking a bit drained herself, Sarah had said earlier, but not for *that* reason, she thought now in determined rejection of any such idea. So she was a few days late. It wasn't exactly the first time. Even allowing for the one or two occasions when Zac had neglected to use a condom, she'd been safeguarded by the Pill, anyway.

Leo received her call with obvious relief. 'I thought you'd been in an accident or something,' he said. 'I was on the verge of ringing the police when Zac called. Don't think about coming back to the office now. There's nothing that can't wait till morning. You go on home to that husband of yours.'

Given a choice, Jessica would have preferred to return to work, but Leo was going to think it very strange if she insisted on it. It seemed insensitive on the face of it to depart the hospital without saying goodbye to Sarah after all they'd gone through together, reluctant though she was to face the questions Brady no doubt had ready by now. There was nothing wrong in her and his wife having lunch together. He and Zac were the ones with the problem.

She found the three of them alone in the pleasant bedroom that was to be Sarah's for the next few days while she acclimatised herself to being a mother. Brady had already acquainted himself with the details of their meeting. He unbent enough to offer his thanks for the speed with which Jessica had acted.

'Naturally, I'd have preferred to be here myself,' he said. The gaze he rested on the baby now sleeping soundly in the crib beside the bed was as proud as any new father's would be. 'A real Prescott, isn't he? Grandfather will be delighted with him!'

'I'm sure your grandmother will be too,' Jessica felt bound to observe. 'I spoke to Zac just now. He got back an hour ago.' It was somewhat less than the truth, but she said it anyway. 'He sends his congratulations.'

'Tell him thanks.' Brady had reverted to the hard-headed character she'd known in Dorset at the mention of Zac's name. 'You'll be wanting to get back home yourself after all this.'

She'd heard subtler hints, Jessica thought drily. She caught Sarah's eye, answering the appeal therein with a smile. 'It's certainly been an eventful afternoon! I'll talk to you on the phone tomorrow, when you're rested.'

She made her escape, glad to be away from the man she found so hard to like. His concern seemed to be more with his grandfather's response to the news than his wife's welfare right now. Sarah looked in dire need of sleep.

It took her nearly an hour to get home. The taxi dropped her at the entrance to the mews, leaving her to dash to number eleven in the sudden heavy downpour that had been threatening for the past half hour. Minus an umbrella, and wearing only a lightweight suit, she was soaked in seconds, her hair forming chestnut corkscrews as the curl took over. Zac came out from the sitting room as she opened the outer door. He viewed her bedraggled figure with unthrilled eyes.

'You better get those things off before you get chilled,' he said.

'I'll make you a hot drink,' called Barbara from the kitchen.

'Don't bother,' she called back. 'I'm fine. I'll be down in a few minutes,' she added to Zac. 'Do you want to stay in, or go out for dinner?'

'We'll go out,' he said, retaining the same level tones.

Jessica headed up the spiral staircase. Reaching the bedroom, she stripped off to the skin, and took a quick shower, then donned fresh underwear and drew on a pair of black, lace-topped stockings to go with the hip-skimming little black dress she fished from the wardrobe.

Her hair she left to dry naturally, after running a brush over it. A swift stroke of a mascara brush over her lashes, a dash of lipstick, and she was ready. Despite the lipstick, her face in the mirror looked colourless. She brushed on some blusher, but it seemed to fade away immediately. Imagination, she told herself brusquely. Any more, and she'd finish up looking like a china doll!

Barbara had gone by the time she got downstairs.

Turning to Zac, Jess asked, 'Shall you be going to see the new arrival?'

'I'd doubt Brady would look too favourably on a visit from me,' Zac returned drily. 'I don't imagine he was any too pleased to know you'd been there at the birth when he couldn't be.'

Jessica lifted her shoulders. 'Understandable. Not that he made it all that obvious. He was just glad someone was with Sarah when it began. He's beautiful. The baby, I mean. They're calling him Henry, after his grandfather.'

'Naturally.' Zac studied her with a certain cynicism. 'Made you feel a little broody yourself, did it?'

Her laugh was forced. 'I can think babies are lovely without necessarily wanting one. It's a lifetime commitment.'

'And you don't see us being together that long?'

Green eyes sought grey, unable to penetrate the depths. 'Do you?' she challenged.

'Why not? Marriages have succeeded on far less than we have in common. Maybe a baby wouldn't be such a bad idea?'

'Especially if it put you back on a par with Brady.' Jessica shook her head forcefully. 'I've told you before, I've no intention of having a baby just to satisfy your grandfather. He might have the two of you in the palm of his hand, but he doesn't have me!'

'Fair enough.' Zac sounded remarkably calm about it. 'So we carry on the way we are for as long as it lasts. Where do you want to eat tonight?'

The swift change of subject left her floundering for a moment. She pulled herself together. 'Anywhere. I don't mind.'

'The Minotaur, then.'

Eating out was the last thing Jessica felt like. Eating at all, in fact. Right now, bed and sleep offered the greatest inducement.

Whatever Zac's inner feelings, he appeared his usual self on the surface the rest of the evening. The problem at the Lyon end had been ironed out without too much difficulty, he said. He didn't mention how he'd passed the previous evening, and Jessica didn't ask. It wasn't outside the bounds of possibility that he'd simply had dinner at the hotel.

Perhaps with their earlier conversation in mind, Zac took care to use protection that night. His ardour was certainly no less for it though. Jessica responded as always, losing herself in the passionate caresses, in the feel of the lean, hard body, the power in his loins. As long as they had this, she could deal with the rest, she told herself on the edge of sleep.

She rang Sarah as promised the following morning, finding her exactly as she had left her the day before.

'Life's absolutely wonderful!' the young mother exclaimed. 'I can't wait to get home with him, and show him off to everybody! Brady insisted on my having some help. Not a full-time nanny exactly, but she'll be there several hours a day.' She laughed. 'I think he's afraid I might find the whole thing too much for me and leave the poor little mite to fend for himself. As if I'd even consider it! You must come over to see us when we're home. Zac too. It's high time he and that husband of mine got together, if only socially.'

'We will,' Jessica promised, putting her doubts on that score aside. 'Give Richard a kiss for me.'

'Everything all right?' asked Leo, emerging from the inner office as she put the phone down. 'You look a bit tired this morning.'

'Never tell a woman she looks tired,' Jessica returned lightly. 'It's like saying she's looking old!'

'Hardly germane at your age.' He smiled back. 'Too many late nights, maybe? Zac doesn't strike me as a man content to don a pair of slippers and watch TV of an evening.'

'You're right,' she said, still on the same light note. 'He's far from ready to settle down to domesticity. Me too, for that matter.'

'Well, providing you're both of the same mind, there's nothing to worry about. My marriage might have lasted a lot longer than it did if we'd shared the same outlook on life. I wanted kids, Christine saw them as too much of a tie. Something we should have gone into before we took the plunge, I suppose, but the subject never came up.'

Jessica kept a tight rein on her emotions as she gave him the file he asked for. So she was looking a little off-colour. Hardly a cause for concern on its own.

Except that it wasn't on its own, of course. She was more than a week late. Still not such a lot, but she'd never fluctuated by that much before.

Suspicion became certainty the very next morning when she was struck by a sudden wave of nausea on rising. She made it to the bathroom just in time, viewing her pale face and lack-lustre eyes through the mirror in wry acceptance. Zac had already gone down, which was some relief. She was going to need to come to terms with this herself before telling him. Not that his reaction was likely to be a bad one with his grandfather still pulling the strings.

Women were at something of an advantage when not looking on top form in having the use of make-up. Jessica applied a light foundation, and took extra care with her eyes to combat the lack of sparkle. The result wasn't perfect, but she doubted if Zac would notice any difference.

Breakfast finished, he was on his second cup of coffee by the time she got downstairs, his attention concentrated on the morning newspaper.

'I was beginning to think you'd decided to go back to bed,' he commented without looking up. 'You'd better get a move on if you want a lift in. I've an early appointment. The coffee's fresh, and there's bread already in the toaster.'

Jessica fancied neither, but crying off breakfast altogether was hardly likely to go unnoticed. She made the toast, and spread a little marmalade, unable to face even the thought of butter. One sip of coffee was enough to convince her that drinking the rest would be tantamount to announcing the condition she was already taking as definite. She was glad she'd only half filled the cup to start with.

'Are you likely to be going away again in the near future?' she asked.

'There's nothing on the immediate agenda,' he said. There was a slight drawing together of the dark brows as he looked across at her, but if he noted anything untoward in her appearance, he made no comment. 'Why?'

Jessica shrugged. 'I just wondered.'

'Thinking about that proper honeymoon I promised you, by any chance?' he queried. 'Unfortunately, this isn't the best time to go to the Maldives. It's the start of their rainy season. Plenty of other places, though.'

Jessica stirred herself, shaking her head emphatically. 'I didn't mean that at all. In fact, I'd forgotten all about it!'

Regard enigmatic, he said, 'So think about it. I like to keep my promises. Just name the place, or places, you most fancy seeing.'

'I can't!' Her tone was too abrupt; she took steps to soften the rejection. 'I mean, I can't take time off now after just starting the job.'

'You don't have to do the damned job at all!' he declared with sudden force.

Jessica firmed her jaw. 'I know that. I *want* to do it.' For as long as possible, she tagged on mentally. She swallowed as nausea stirred again, pushing back her chair. 'We'd better get moving if you want to make that appointment.'

Zac made no further reference to the subject. He didn't speak much at all on the way to Holbourn. He'd pick her up at five-thirty if nothing cropped up in the meantime, he said on dropping her off.

The day was fraught. Jessica wasn't sick again, but she

felt decidedly queasy. It could take as long as three months for the hormones to sort themselves out, she'd read somewhere. The nausea could apparently be relieved by medication, which called for a visit to a doctor. Zac would have one, of course, but she wasn't ready yet to give him the news. Not while there was still the slightest chance that it was a false alarm.

She slipped out at lunchtime and bought a pregnancy testing kit, then spent fifteen minutes in the cloakroom nerving herself to do the test. The result proved positive, removing the last doubt from her mind.

Standing there, gazing at the strip, Jessica was aware of a stirring deep down in the very centre of her being. Emotional, not physical, she realised. New life was already growing inside her, minuscule at present, but destined to become a fully developed human being. Whatever else happened, this child was going to be loved and protected, she vowed.

Having resolved to tell Zac on the way home, she was dashed when he phoned to say he was going to be late. He didn't say why, and she didn't ask, unwilling to give any leeway to the thought that had sprung in the back of her mind. The news would keep. In fact, a little more time to assimilate it properly herself wouldn't go amiss.

Zac took it for granted that she called for a taxi to transport her to and from the office on the occasions he was unable to do it himself. At peak times, Jessica found the tube just as quick. She had never suffered from claustrophobia in her life, but tonight, strap hanging on the packed train, she felt everything closing in on her. Hormonal again, she reckoned, thankful to emerge. Taxis might be preferable after all.

The time was going to come when she had to give the job up altogether, of course. Sitting behind a desk with a front the size Sarah's had been would prove impossible.

Whether Zac would still find her desirable when she looked like that was open to question.

She made herself a snack when he hadn't turned up by eight o'clock. Not because she felt like eating, but because she had a responsibility towards the life growing inside her. By nine she was beginning to doubt, by ten to definitely suspect. When he finally arrived at half-past, she was ready to let fly.

'Where do you think I've been?' he responded curtly. 'With another woman?'

The directness of it took her aback for a moment, but only for a moment. Attack had always been the best means of defence.

'Why not?' she challenged. 'We've been married a whole six and a half weeks! A long time for a man as used as you are to playing the field!'

One dark brow lifted sardonically. 'If I've given the impression I'm bored with you, I must try to do better. If you want the truth, I've been seeing an old friend. Male, as it happens. In town for the one night before heading back to New York.'

Jessica rallied her waning forces. 'So why didn't you tell me that when you phoned?'

'Because I was already late for a meeting. I could have got my secretary to phone you with more detail, of course, but I didn't think that would go down too well. Was I wrong?'

'No,' she said after a moment.

Zac eyed her dispassionately. 'You look tired. You should have gone to bed.'

'I'm fine.' It was an effort to keep her tone from reflecting her feelings. She tried a new track. 'I phoned Sarah this morning. They're both still doing well. She wants us to go over when she's home.'

'She might, Brady certainly won't.'

The anger returned full force. 'It's about time the two of you started pulling together!' she snapped. 'You're like dogs fighting over a bone—with your grandfather on the sideline urging you on! You're cousins, for God's sake!'

'Even closer than that.' Zac was angry himself, his eyes like cold steel. 'My father had an affair with Brady's mother. He was the result. That makes him my half brother.'

Jessica gazed at him in shock for several seconds before she found her voice again. 'Does he know?'

'Yes, he knows. His mother told him the truth after our fathers were killed, and he told me.'

Mind whirling, Jessica said slowly, 'Your mother had no idea?'

'Oh, yes. She'd been aware of it from the start.'

'But she stayed with him? Your father, I mean.'

'She stayed for my sake. I was about six months old when Brady was born.'

Green eyes widened. 'Your father had the affair while your mother was pregnant with you?'

'So it would appear.' Zac looked as if he was beginning to regret having begun this. 'Some men find pregnancy a sexual turn-off. And no, I'm not finding excuses for him, but his sister-in-law—my aunt—obviously made herself readily available.'

Jessica's head was lowered, the lump in her throat hard to swallow. If his father had found pregnancy a sexual turn-off, then it was likely that he might too. Not a brilliant outlook for a marriage lacking anything else to hold it together—apart from those damned shares!

'Lousy situation though it is, I don't think you and Brady should allow it to colour your lives to the extent you do,' she said thickly. 'Your grandfather doesn't help.' She looked up as the thought struck her. 'He did know?'

Zac gave a short laugh. 'He didn't at the time. If he

had, he'd have cut Dad off pronto. Brady told him within days of hearing it himself. Hence the added pressure on me to make good.'

'You can't possibly be blamed for what your father did!'

'As his son, I'm expected to atone for it.'

'That's unfair!'

'That's life,' Zac returned drily. 'We've been asked to make another visit, by the way.'

'Asked,' she flashed, 'or commanded?'

The shrug was brief. 'Tell it the way you see it. Whatever his faults, I'm fond of the old devil. Even more so of my grandmother. She's devoted a lifetime to him. The least I can do is spend the occasional weekend.' He paused, eyes veiled now as he regarded her. 'I can't force you to come with me, of course. That has to be up to you.'

'But it will hardly do your image any good if I don't.'

The sarcasm left him unmoved. 'Probably not. Anyway, it's been a long day. I'm going to bed. Don't stay up too long. You look a bit washed out yourself.'

He was gone before she could comment. Not that there was a great deal she could have said other than to tell him the reason she looked washed out, as he so tactfully put it. Her pregnancy would certainly enhance his stature in Henry Prescott's eyes, but how would he regard it himself? A baby was going to alter their whole way of living.

He was asleep when she finally went up, lying on his back, his breathing deep and even. Many men snored in that position, she'd heard, but she didn't even have that much to find fault with.

The night was warm, and he'd pushed the duvet aside. Nude, as always in bed, his body gleamed like bronze in the soft light from the bedside lamp he'd left burning. Jessica studied the strong, clean lines, eyes traversing a route downwards over the broad chest with its tapering V of hair to the hard-packed midriff and narrowed hipline, the firmly muscled thighs enclosing the very essence of his masculinity.

Even dormant, he was well-endowed. She touched her tongue to lips gone dry at the image in her mind's eye of how he looked when he was fully aroused. She wanted him desperately, but she wasn't prepared to waken him. Not the way things were. He would have to know eventually, of course, but not yet. It was hardly as if she was going to give birth tomorrow.

CHAPTER NINE

CONCEALING the nausea which struck her every morning over the following couple of weeks wasn't easy. Fortunately, it didn't last long, and she was able to eat breakfast as normal. Zac appeared to notice nothing untoward, at any rate.

The doctor she finally signed on with confirmed the pregnancy, and arranged for her to start ante-natal clinic at twelve weeks. If he wondered why her husband hadn't accompanied her, he kept the thought to himself. It was even possible, Jessica supposed, that he took the 'Mrs' as a self-bestowed title.

Zac hadn't mentioned his grandparents again, and she had no intention of bringing the subject up. Her blood boiled whenever she thought about the way Henry Prescott had reacted to news of his son's wrongdoing. Zac had obviously trodden a very dangerous line in holding out against the old man's views as long as he had. As the major shareholder in the company still, his grandfather had to have been in a position to make life very difficult for him, to say the least. Some might say he could have walked away from it, but why should he land everything in his half-brother's lap?

Life went on apace. They ate out most evenings, twice by invitation. While coping quite adequately on the surface with the hormonal changes taking place in her body, Jessica found the very thought of giving a dinner party of their own stressful. The dining room wasn't big enough to hold more than six round the table in any real comfort, she protested when Zac said it was time they returned the

130

hospitality, and she doubted her ability to prepare a meal of the standard expected anyway.

Zac shot down the first objection by saying they could split it into two parties, the second by suggesting a catering company could supply a meal all ready to serve on both occasions.

'As a married man, it's time I started returning the hospitality I've enjoyed as a bachelor,' he said. 'If you're finding this place a bit too compact for comfort, we can always move somewhere larger.'

'That wasn't what I meant,' Jessica denied. 'I love it here! All right,' she added on a sudden reckless surge, 'Make it next Saturday, and I'll even do the cooking myself!'

It was a Saturday today. They were lazing over coffee in the sitting room with the weekend newspapers and magazines. Zac studied her reflectively where she sat with feet curled up under her on the sofa.

'Not all it's cracked up to be, is it?' he said on a wry note.

The green eyes lifted to his were cautious. 'What isn't?'

'Marriage.'

Jessica felt her heart take a plunge. It was all she could do to keep her voice steady. 'It depends on the expectations, I suppose. Ours wasn't exactly what you might call a match made in heaven to start with.'

The expression that flitted across the firm masculine features was come and gone too quickly for definition. His voice was equally steady. 'Maybe not. Still, it has its compensations. Although those are in pretty short supply at present. Nature's way, I know,' he added before she could voice the reply he obviously heard coming, 'but no less frustrating for the average male.'

He returned to his paper, his face closed against her.

Jessica resisted the urge to apologise for the dig. He was the one who'd started it, she excused herself.

The realisation that he'd taken her lack of response to him these last few nights to be due to her period was something of a surprise considering how far past her due date she was. Yet how many men kept an actual tally, if it came to that? If it had crossed his mind at all, he would probably have taken it that she had an irregular cycle.

Her failure to feel any degree of desire for him at present was explained in the book she'd bought on pregnancy. Some women suffered a lowering of libido in the initial stages, it seemed. In a normal marriage, with love to fall back on, it wouldn't matter as much, but deprived of the only consolation he had for his loss of freedom, a healthy, virile man like Zac might find the temptation to look elsewhere for solace too great to resist.

So tell him the truth, her inner voice urged. He was hardly going to look on the news with disfavour, taking his grandfather's views into account. Except that she hated the mere thought of those views having any kind of bearing on his reaction, she admitted wryly.

At least his assumption gave her a few days' breathing space. If her urges failed to return to normal, she would just have to put on an act. As Zac himself had pointed out, women had no physical evidence of arousal to produce.

Despite their differences, the day passed pleasantly enough. Zac had booked theatre tickets for the evening, followed by a late supper at Quaglino's. The last thing Jessica felt like was eating at that hour, but she made a valiant effort. The least she could do, she considered, when he'd gone to such trouble to arrange things.

'This time last year, I'd have thought myself lucky to be treated to supper at the local fish bar,' she commented,

not entirely in jest. 'I certainly never imagined myself in
a place like this. You're used to it, of course.'

Zac gave a light shrug. 'I wouldn't call it one of my
regular haunts. Left to my own devices, I'd plump for a
good pub meal washed down with a pint of best bitter.'

'Were you often?' she asked. 'Left to your own devices,
I mean.'

The shrug came again. 'You can't burn the candle at
both ends every night of the week, and still turn in an
adequate performance during the day. Anyway, I'm past
dancing the night away. Vertically, at any rate,' he tagged
on with the wicked sparkle Jessica had so missed these
past weeks.

'Do men ever think of anything else?' she teased, responding to the sudden uplift in her own spirits as she
looked into the grey eyes lit by the soft glow from the
table lamp.

He studied her for a moment before answering, taking
in the peach-skinned oval of her face within its frame of
chestnut spirals. His smile played havoc on her heart
strings.

'Depends on the incentive. I'd defy any man to look at
you and think about cricket scores.'

Desire rocketed through her: all the stronger, it seemed,
for the hiatus. It brought both relief and dismay. The former because she'd been afraid of never regaining the feeling, the latter because she'd led him to believe her una-
vailable for the present.

'Look at me like *that*, and I'm liable to forget where
we are,' he said softly. 'I think I'd better call for the bill.
And no, I haven't forgotten,' he added.

Jessica fought a battle with herself in the taxi going
back to the mews. All she had to do was admit the truth.
The baby wasn't going to go away; she wouldn't want it
to go away! Tell him now and get it over with, then they

could continue from there. The marriage might not be perfect, but how many were?

The words just wouldn't come. Even when he took her by the hand and led her straight upstairs on reaching the house, she found it impossible. She clung to him as he kissed her, blotting out everything but the here and now.

They undressed each other, one garment at a time. Jessica pressed her legs together instinctively when he slid his hands down over her smooth curves, but he made no attempt to touch her there, caressing the rounded hemispheres of her behind as his lips followed the line of her jaw to reach the tender lobe of her ear.

The shudder running through her was no pretence. She closed a hand about him, seeking to give him the same pleasure he was giving her. He said something guttural under his breath as she began the movement, his whole body rigid with tension.

'Not yet,' he murmured against her skin.

She desisted at once in recognition of how close to climaxing he'd come at her mere touch. Her hands slid behind the dark head as he moved on down the line of her throat to find her breast, her fingers curling into the thickness of his hair at the exquisite sensation engendered by his flickering tongue. She was taking everything and giving nothing—and all because of her reluctance to tell him what he had a right to know. She should do it now. This moment!

She didn't, because her mouth still refused to form the words. The thought itself faded as Zac laid her on the bed and began kissing his way down the full length of her body. Jessica had never realised just how many erogenous zones the body possessed until now, and he knew them all. By the time he finished with her she couldn't have found the strength to lift a finger.

It took his disappearance into the bathroom to bring her

back to life. Lying there in the darkness, she tried to sort out her tangled emotions. Tonight Zac had proved himself capable of a selflessness that stirred her to the depths. For a man to sublimate his own needs that way, there surely had to be some feeling other than just the physical on his part. Whether it was enough to survive the realisation that his altruism had been unnecessary was something else.

She turned out the bedside lights before he came back to bed, steeling herself when he slid in beside her. She'd tried out a dozen ways of saying it over the last few minutes, but when it came to the crunch she found herself tongue-tied still.

Zac drew her to him to kiss the tip of her nose. The brush of silk against her lower body proclaimed his use of pyjamas trousers.

'A temporary measure only,' he said on a humorous note.

Leaving an arm about her, he turned onto his back. Jessica yearned to press her lips to his bare chest, to feel the flat hard muscle beneath the wiry curl of hair and fill her nostrils with his clean masculine scent. She didn't because it wouldn't be fair. Not while he was still labouring under the same illusion.

It was a long time before she slept.

Sarah's call on the Sunday morning was answered by Zac. His response to her greeting was easy enough, his reaction to the invitation that Jessica gathered was being issued surprisingly lacking in reticence.

'We'll see you this afternoon then,' he concluded.

'Hard to refuse when Sarah's doing the asking,' he acknowledged, replacing the receiver. 'She's a nice kid. Far too good for Brady!'

'She doesn't think so,' Jessica returned mildly.

Zac slanted a lip. 'Ah, well, they say love is blind!

We'll have lunch somewhere, and then head out to Sevenoaks.'

'We can have lunch here,' Jessica suggested. 'There's a ready-cooked chicken in the fridge, and plenty of salad ingredients. Unless you'd rather go out, of course?'

'I thought you would,' he said after a moment. 'You've never given the impression of being very enamoured of playing the housewife.'

'I'm not,' she agreed lightly. 'Not as a full-time job, at any rate. But I've no objection to preparing the odd meal, and chicken salad hardly calls for any great culinary expertise.'

Zac's smile was brief. 'True enough. Salad it is, then.'

Jessica had spoken the truth just now, but it was an attitude that was going to have to change to a great degree with a baby to care for, came the thought. Something she would just have to tackle when the time came. The problem right now was how and when to impart the news.

Large and imposing with its mock Tudor frontage, the Sevenoaks house was the antithesis of their own abode, though Jessica had no doubts about her preference. Brady made little effort to conceal the fact that it hadn't been his idea to invite them over.

Richard Henry was already developing a distinct personality. Zac slanted a smile at the resounding raspberry blown in his direction.

'A real chip off the old block!' he remarked.

'Wind,' declared the child's mother on a practical note.

'We went down to Whitegates last weekend,' said Brady. 'Grandfather's very taken with him. He was put out that you two hadn't been down again,' he added on a sly note. 'Not that I personally blame you. I'd resent it like hell if he'd played the same game with me.'

'I might not have appreciated the method,' Zac returned calmly, 'but the only difference it made was in time.'

'As a matter of fact,' put in Jessica without forethought, 'we were planning on going next weekend.'

'They'll both be delighted to see you,' said Sarah before Brady could make any further comment. 'Why don't you and Zac take a stroll round the garden, darling, while Jessica and I have a woman to woman chat?' she added ingenuously.

Neither man looked enthused by the idea, but they went anyway. Sarah gave a cheeky grin as the drawing room door closed in their wake.

'That should give us at least half an hour to relax. Try to ignore Brady's little digs. He still finds it hard to accept, even after seven years.' She paused, quirking an eyebrow. 'You do know about it by now?'

'If you mean about them being half brothers, yes,' Jessica acknowledged. 'I don't imagine it's been easy for either of them.'

'At least Zac can claim legitimacy. Brady feels he was deprived. His mother should never have told him the truth. Not after all those years.'

Jessica could agree with that. 'Were they good friends when they believed they were just cousins, do you know?' she asked.

'Certainly better than they are now, I'd think, although they've such different temperaments, I'd doubt they were ever very close. Brady doesn't have much of a sense of humour, as you might have gathered.' Sarah was smiling as she said it. 'He considers Zac's approach to life lacking in gravity. Since he found out what his grandfather had been up to, he suspects him of marrying you just to secure his inheritance too. He's wrong, of course. Anybody with half an eye can see how the two of you feel about one another.'

Jessica gave a smile by way of response, wishing she could be as sure even of her own feelings these days.

'Don't put off having a baby for too long though,' Sarah tagged on. 'It's what marriage is all about.' She laughed. 'Brady thinks a maximum of two is the ideal family, but I want at least four. It will be interesting to see which of us wins out.'

If strength of mind was any criteria, Jessica knew which way she'd place her bets.

The men returned from the garden scarcely more communicative than when they'd left. Although she could appreciate the reason for their lack of camaraderie, it was time, Jessica thought, that they made an effort to come to terms with it. Not that there was anything she, or Sarah either, could do about it. It was entirely up to them.

Sarah wanted them to stay on for dinner. Zac declined on the grounds that they had a prior engagement.

'Why bother lying about it?' Jessica asked when they were in the car. 'Brady wouldn't have wanted us to stay on.'

'It wasn't Brady doing the asking,' he said. 'And what makes you so sure I was lying about it?'

She gave him a swift glance. 'Weren't you?'

'As a matter of fact, no. I thought, considering the weather, you might like to eat outside at a riverside inn I know.'

'That can hardly be called a prior engagement.'

'It can when I'd already planned on doing it.' It was Zac's turn to slant a glance: a somewhat intolerant one. 'If you don't want to go, just say so!'

'I do.' She wasn't all that keen, if the truth were known, but the hairsplitting had irritated him enough without cocking a snook at the offer. What was wrong with her anyway? Most women would be only too delighted to have a husband who planned surprises.

She knew what was wrong with her, of course. Sarah's

unallayed contentment with and confidence in her marriage aroused a bitter envy.

She stole another glance at Zac, senses stirred as always by the strength of character in the chiselled profile. What was she carping about? He was everything a woman could want in a man!

Everything a lot of women *would* want still, married or not, came the rider. The question being just how seriously he regarded the vows he'd taken in that church.

'Sorry,' she proffered. 'It's a great idea, really it is!'

'No need to go overboard,' he said drily. 'It's just an inn. We'll no doubt be sharing it with a load more. It might be a good idea to get a reasonably early night tonight.'

He was putting her touchiness down to her condition, Jessica assumed. Which it probably was, to a great extent, although not quite the condition he had in mind. The longer she left the telling, the harder it was going to be, but she still couldn't bring herself to make the move.

Later, she promised herself, after she'd gained Dutch courage via a couple of drinks. Come what may, it had to be done tonight.

The inn was a well-preserved, sixteenth-century delight, with low ceilings, wooden beams and fine cooking. The place was fully booked, but an extra table was set up for them on the riverside terrace beneath a loggia overhung with grapevine.

'One of the perks of the frequent customer,' said Zac. 'Although it's weeks since I was in last.'

'It has to be at least a couple of months,' Jessica agreed. 'I can understand why you like it so much though. The atmosphere is wonderful!'

'You should see the place at Christmas when they go the whole traditional hog and roast the meat on a spit over the fire. Christmas day, the staff dress in period costume. Some of the clientele too.'

'Did you ever do it?' she asked.

'Only under duress, and then only the once. I usually go up to Scotland for the break.'

'That must please your mother,' she commented, wondering who had provided the duress.

'It pleases me too.' There was a pause, a change of tone. 'Were you serious about going down to Dorset next weekend?'

Jessica hadn't been at the time, but backing out now was beyond her. 'Why not?' she said. 'I'd like to see your grandmother again.'

'But not Grandfather.'

'Can you blame me for that?'

'No.' Both face and voice were expressionless now. 'I can't blame you for any of it. Just try to remember he's an old man with attitudes probably implanted in him by his own father.'

His gaze shifted as someone came up behind Jessica, expression altering. 'Fleur! Good to see you!'

'And you,' replied a husky female voice. 'Patrick suggested we come out and ask if you minded us joining you—yours being the only table with seats going spare.'

'Of course.' Zac got to his feet to pull out the chair at his side. 'Take this one.'

The woman moved round the table to do so, leaving her companion to slide into the chair next to Jessica. 'Sorry about this,' said the man apologetically.

'It's no problem,' Zac assured him. Face composed, he said, 'I'd like you to meet my wife. Fleur Reddington, Jessica.'

The expression in the newcomer's eyes belied the words of congratulation on her lips. An extremely attractive blonde around Leonie's age, she had been a great deal closer to Zac in the past than a mere friend, Jessica reckoned.

The man with her was introduced as Toby Barstow. To Jessica, it was obvious that he sensed the same thing she did, although it didn't appear to bother him unduly. Neither should she allow it to bother her, she knew. She was well aware that Zac had been no monk. Fleur probably wasn't the only old flame she was destined to meet.

What conversation there was between the two of them over the evening was stilted. Fleur concentrated the majority of her attention on Zac, reminiscing about people and places and times that left Toby as obviously on the sidelines as Jessica herself. The affair had to have lasted several weeks, if not months, for so much to have gone on, she assessed.

Zac was quiet on the way home. Regretting his lost freedom, Jessica suspected. Right now, she regretted hers. If she'd never met Zac she would be out there living her own life. Perhaps with her own place by now, even if only a bed-sit. Instead she was stuck in a marriage that had never been intended, carrying a baby she couldn't bring herself to declare. What kind of a life was that?

Zac made no attempt to make love to her again the way he had the previous night, although he did kiss her goodnight. Lying there sleepless herself, she could tell from his breathing that he was awake too. Meeting up with Fleur tonight had stirred memories he was apparently finding difficulty in casting from mind. If he'd loved the woman he would surely have married her, but that didn't mean she left him untouched.

The medication provided by the doctor had eased the early morning sickness. All the same, it was becoming an increasing effort to face going to work.

Her own fault, Jessica acknowledged ruefully on the

way in next morning. Unlike so many women in her condition, she was under no financial pressure to carry on with her job. Once Zac knew—and it couldn't be much longer—he would probably insist that she give it up anyway.

It was the morning cup of coffee that let her down. Up to now, she'd had no problem with it; this particular morning, the very smell of it suddenly turned her stomach, calling for a speedy retreat.

She returned to the office pale faced, to be greeted by Leo with a dawning certainty.

'You're pregnant, aren't you?' he said.

Jessica bit back the denial that sprang instinctively to her lips. She spread her hands in a wry gesture. 'How did you guess?'

'The way you've looked one or two mornings started me suspecting,' he admitted. 'I'm surprised Zac's willing to let you carry on working. I know how I'd feel.'

'I've hardly been here five minutes,' Jessica responded. 'I can't just walk out on you. I wouldn't even want to!'

'It's surely what's best for the baby that counts,' he said. 'You too, if it comes to that. There's no reason for you to even serve notice in the circumstances. I can always call on the agencies for a temp.'

Jessica shook her head. 'There's no need. Not yet, at any rate. I prefer to keep occupied.'

'Well, I can't pretend I wouldn't be sorry to lose you too soon,' he acknowledged. 'Zac's a very lucky man!'

Jessica passed off the moment as best she could. Having another man know she was pregnant before Zac himself was hardly what she would have chosen, but it was done now. She'd put things right tonight.

The call from his secretary came just after she returned from lunch. Mr Prescott had been called away on urgent business and would be gone overnight, said the woman.

He'd tried to reach her on her mobile, but had found it switched off. He could be reached by mobile himself should the need arise.

The need, Jessica considered depressedly, had already arisen. Not that she intended indulging it. Hard as she tried to keep it at bay, the suspicion was there. Coming so soon after the meeting with an old flame, the urgent overnight business took on certain undertones. He hadn't been getting much satisfaction from her lately, after all.

She went home by taxi. Supper consisted of the bit of chicken salad left over from the day before. She needed to eat rather more substantially for the baby's sake, she knew, but she couldn't have forced another morsel down her throat at present.

Zac rang at nine. He was dealing with some problem that had arisen with one of their northern subsidiaries, he said. There would be another day of it tomorrow, but he hoped to be back by evening.

Jessica could hear voices in the background—one of them definitely a woman's—and the clink of glasses. If he was in a hotel bedroom, it could be coming from the television, of course. *If* being the operative word. She flatly refused to ask where he was.

It was a long night made even longer by the thunderstorm that raged through a good two hours of it. She was heavy-eyed and enervated in the morning. She even contemplated taking advantage of her condition to call in sick, but conscience wouldn't allow it. Sitting around here thinking about something that might not even have happened wasn't going to do her much good, in any case.

Leo was all solicitation. She mustn't do *any* lifting and carrying, he admonished on catching her attempting to shift a filing cabinet to secure a paper that had fallen down behind. Zac would never forgive him, he declared, if anything should go wrong.

Which was all very fine, but left Jessica feeling more of a liability than an asset. Working the three or four months she planned might prove too much for both of them, she reckoned.

Zac got back around eight after a journey he described as hellish.

'I ate on the way,' he said when Jessica asked. 'What I need right now is a good stiff whisky!' He moved across to the drinks tray, saying over a shoulder, 'How about you?'

'Nothing, thanks,' she said.

'Not even a glass of wine?' He glanced back at her when she repeated the refusal, brows lifting quizzically. 'On the wagon?'

Now was the time, but she let the moment pass. 'I just don't feel like it.'

The grey eyes sharpened a little as he studied her. 'Not sickening for something, I hope?'

'Not fancying a drink is hardly a sign of ill health,' she retorted a little more shortly than intended. 'I'm absolutely fine!'

'Good.' He sounded short himself.

He poured the whisky, added soda, and took a good long pull before bringing the glass back to take a seat on the sofa where she was sitting herself, stretching his legs with a sigh of relief.

'Nice to relax at last. It's been a tough day!'

'But you got things sorted?' she said.

'Eventually, yes.'

'The hotel okay?'

'Fine.' He slanted a curious glance. 'Why?'

Jessica lifted her shoulders. 'Just taking an interest. It's what wives are supposed to do, isn't it?'

'Only if they are. Interested, I mean. You strike me as

talking for the sake of talking.' The pause was brief, his gaze penetrating. 'What's wrong?'

Another opportunity, but she didn't take it. The devil driving her was too powerful to be diverted. 'What could possibly be wrong?' she responded. 'I have a handsome husband, a lovely home, no financial concerns—what more could any woman ask for?'

'Obviously a great deal,' he said. 'I'm sorry if you find life unsatisfactory. I can't claim to be exactly fulfilled by it myself.'

She was hearing nothing she wasn't already aware of, Jessica acknowledged, but it still hurt. It was only the thought of the baby that kept her from flinging the word divorce in his face.

'I'm sorry too,' she said bitterly. 'Sorry we ever met. Your grandfather has a lot to answer for!'

'That I can agree with.' There was a lengthy pause, punctuated by the seemingly magnified tick of the carriage clock on the mantle. When he spoke again it was with control. 'I gather you won't be going down there this weekend.'

'That's all you're really bothered about, isn't it?' Jessica shot back. 'Well, you needn't worry! I'll keep up the pretence!'

She made to get up, to be brought up short by the hand that seized her elbow. Zac was blazingly, furiously angry, the skin stretched taut over hard cheekbones.

'You've known the score all along,' he gritted. 'What the hell brought this on?'

'The realisation that I'm married to a man I not only don't love, but don't even like!' she snapped back, totally losing it. 'Oh, you're very good at sex, I'll grant you that. But then you should be, given the practice you've had!'

'You're not so dusty yourself, considering your lack of

it,' came the biting response. 'That's if Paul really was
your first and only experience! For all...'

He broke off abruptly, a look of self-disgust wiping the
anger from his face. The hand grasping her elbow was
withdrawn. 'Forget I said that.'

'Why?' Jessica's voice was ragged. 'If it's what you
believe.'

'It isn't. The idea hadn't even crossed my mind before
now.' Zac had himself under control again, his jaw rigid.
'I thought we had something we could possibly build on.
Just goes to show how wrong you can be about someone.'

Jessica drew a long, uneven breath, struggling to bring
her warring emotions under some semblance of order.
'We both said things we didn't mean,' she got out. 'I do
like you, Zac. Most of the time, at any rate,' she added
in an attempt to bring a touch of humour to the moment.

'That's comforting.' There was no humour at all in the
grey eyes. 'All we need now are the violins, and everything's back to normal.' He got to his feet, shaking his
head when she made to speak. 'I think we've both said
enough for one night. I'm going for a shower.'

Jessica subsided into the cushions as he went from the
room. She felt sick again: emotionally rather than physically. If there had ever been anything to build on, she had
killed it stone dead in these last few minutes.

CHAPTER TEN

A NEAR silent drive to work left Jessica in no frame of mind to give of her best.

'I'm sure it would be better for you to be at home with your feet up, rather than messing around at the office,' Leo remarked diffidently the third time he had to repeat something he'd said.

Jessica donned a smile. 'I object to the "messing around" bit.'

He smiled back reluctantly. 'You know what I mean. If you were my wife, you wouldn't have a choice in the matter!'

'I can't think of anything more boring at the moment than sitting at home with my feet up,' she said. 'There'll be time enough for that later.'

There was going to be time enough for a lot of things, she thought hollowly, turning her attention back to the computer screen. Just not the right ones.

Zac had been in bed when she'd finally geared herself into going upstairs last night. He hadn't spoken. Nor had she. They'd lain there like a couple of strangers. Which was what they were still, in most respects. She had no doubt that she could still make him want her if she put her mind to it, but sex alone couldn't sustain a marriage indefinitely. Whether a baby could remained to be seen.

Leo seemed oddly withdrawn when she returned from lunch. He left almost immediately to keep an appointment he'd apparently forgotten to mention. It would probably be easier on him if she went, Jessica reflected wryly. She was too much of a reminder of how empty his own life was. He had women friends, she knew, but no one special: no one likely, from what she could gather, to give him the family life he craved.

Zac's arrival some ten minutes later was a total shock. One look at his expression was enough to tell her that her secret was out. Only one person could have told him.

Zac's first words confirmed it—if confirmation was needed. 'My wife is pregnant,' he clipped, 'and *I* have to find out from another man!'

'I'm sorry,' she said stiffly. 'I never meant for it to happen like that. What exactly did Leo say?'

'He rang to congratulate me—and to suggest that it might be better if you took an early retirement considering how you've been feeling. Would it be too much to ask how you *have* been feeling?'

The resentment filling her was defensive. 'Sick,' she said with purpose. 'Not all the time, admittedly, but enough to provide a hint for anyone with a modicum of interest. Leo guessed when I couldn't look a cup of coffee in the face a couple of days ago. *You* didn't even notice all those early-morning treks to the bathroom!'

Eyes glittering, Zac drove his hands into trouser pockets. 'You obviously didn't mean me to notice. Just how far on are you?'

'Eight weeks—give or take a few days.'

'*Eight* weeks!'

'I haven't been certain of it that long, of course,' Jessica went on doggedly. 'I did a test a couple of days after Sarah's baby was born. It was positive.'

His voice gained an even rougher edge. 'So why the pretence this past week?'

'It wasn't so much a pretence as an assumption on your part. I've been going through a phase a lot of women apparently go through in the early stages.'

'Really? That was quite a sacrifice you made the other night, then.'

'It wasn't like that,' she protested.

'No? So just when were you planning on telling me? If you planned on telling me at all, that is.'

Jessica drew a harsh breath. 'If you mean was I considering a secret abortion, the idea would never have entered my head!'

'You're saying you really want this baby?' Zac curled a lip when no answer was immediately forthcoming. 'I guess not.'

Voice ragged, she said, 'It isn't a case of wanting or not wanting. I just don't happen to think we're ideal parent material, that's all.'

'So we learn to be. Starting here and now with what's best *for* the baby. Get your things. I'm taking you home. Leo knows about it.'

Green eyes sparked afresh. 'He might, I don't! I'll give notice when I'm good and ready!'

'You're ready now.' Zac wasn't giving an inch. 'I'll pack you out over a shoulder if I have to,' he threatened when she made no move.

In this mood, he was capable of it, Jessica reckoned. Face set, she collected her belongings. She was doing this only because it was easier at the moment, but it wasn't the end of it. She was the one carrying this child; *she* was the one to decide what was what.

The people at work in the outer office viewed the pair of them curiously as they passed. Zac had closed the door on arrival, but it was evident that the sound of raised voices, if not the words themselves, had filtered through. Jessica plastered a smile on her face, though she doubted if it convinced anybody.

Zac had the Jaguar parked on double yellow lines. There was a ticket already tucked beneath the wiper. He tore it out and thrust it into a pocket before sliding behind the wheel to fire the ignition with a vicious flick of a wrist. The traffic, as always, was heavy, the journey to Chelsea a series of stops and starts that hardly improved his state of mind. Jessica stayed silent, gathering herself for the battle to come. There was no way he was going to dictate to her over this. No way!

It was only on hearing the sound of a vacuum on entering the house that either of them remembered it was Wednesday. Barbara greeted them with surprise followed by speculation as she took in the atmosphere between the pair of them.

'Nice to be able to take an afternoon off when the fancy strikes,' she said. 'Going out somewhere?'

'No.' Zac made no attempt to wrap it up. 'You can take the afternoon yourself, Barbara. Paid, naturally.'

The offer was accepted without hesitation. Not that she had a great deal of choice, Jessica reflected. She went through to the kitchen and made herself a coffee while the woman got her things together, needing the caffeine boost. It stayed down this time which was a help.

She was still drinking it when Zac came through. He stood in the doorway, his whole attitude inflexible.

'To get back to what I asked you earlier,' he said. 'When *were* you planning on telling me?'

'When I could gear myself to it,' she rejoined. 'Let's not kid ourselves, Zac. The only real interest you have in becoming a father is that it puts you on a par with Brady in your grandfather's books. Keeping your brother from inheriting control of the company is your main aim in life!'

'One of them maybe. I do have others. And he isn't my brother.'

'Half-brother, then, if we must split hairs. You're neither of you responsible for what happened between your parents. Why can't you just accept it and start trying to work together instead of against each other?'

'Because we're two totally different people,' came the curt reply. 'My father was very much a chip off the old block. Brady takes after them both. Apart from his business sense, that is. Grandfather's retired in name only. He still holds the controlling interest. Give that to Brady, and it's downhill all the way.'

'Something of an exaggeration, surely,' Jessica protested.

The mobile left eyebrow lifted sardonically. 'What would you know about it?' He made a dismissive gesture. 'That's not the issue here, anyway. We have a marriage to salvage—for the baby's sake if nothing else. Taking it you're not averse to physical contact any longer, we can start from there.

'Not now,' he added with cynicism, sensing the rejection already framing on her lips. 'Just how crass do you think I am?' He didn't wait for any reply. 'I'm going back in. You stay here and sort yourself out. Just settle your mind to the fact that you're finished with work yourself.'

He was gone before she could form any further protest. She heard the car start up again, the decreasing sound as he turned out of the mews. If he thought the matter settled, he could think again, she told herself hardily.

Leo was in the office when she rang around four-thirty. He was all apologies.

'I should have minded my own business,' he said. 'It never occurred to me that Zac...'

'That Zac wouldn't know about it yet,' Jessica finished for him. 'I'm the one who should be apologising. I put you in rotten position.'

'Forget it,' he said. The pause was significant. 'Is everything...all right?'

'All sorted,' she assured him. 'I'll see you in the morning.'

'Morning?' He sounded taken aback. 'But I thought…' He paused again, his confusion evident even over the line. 'I think it might be best all round if we called it a day,' he said at length. 'I already contacted the agency.'

Jessica did her best to conceal her feelings. 'I suppose you're right. I wasn't giving the job my full attention.'

'That's not the reason,' he protested. 'You're the best secretary I ever had!'

Her laugh was brittle. 'If I ever need a reference, I'll know where to come. It's been nice knowing you, Leo.'

She rang off before he could say anything further. She should have known, of course, that Zac would make certain he got his way. There were two paths she could take from here: either she spent the coming months keeping him at a distance, or she put some effort into bringing the two of them closer. If this marriage was to stand any chance at all, there was no real choice. Suspicion had to be the first thing to go.

Zac arrived home at six-thirty, looking ready for battle. Her lack of antagonism threw him completely.

'I expected to find you still seething,' he admitted.

Jessica gave a brief smile. 'I've had time to think about it. You were right earlier. The baby has to be the first concern. I'm sorry for the way you had to find out about it.'

'I should have realised,' he said. 'I've been pretty obtuse. I didn't intend this to happen, believe me. I know I've been lax with the precautions once or twice, but it seemed a safe enough indulgence with you on the Pill.'

'The Pill isn't a hundred per cent safeguard even taken without any gaps. I've been careless too on occasion, so if any blame is to be attached at all, it should probably be mine.'

Zac regarded her with enigmatic expression. 'Leaving all that aside, how do you really feel about it?'

'Being pregnant?' Jessica gave another faint smile. 'I'm getting used to it. Planned or not, your grandfather is going to be pleased when we tell him this weekend.'

'That can wait.' His tone was suddenly decisive. 'You need a break. We both do. Any preferences?'

Jessica shook her head, trying not to read too much into too little. 'Can you find the time?' she asked.

'I'll make the time. Nobody's indispensable. I'll get onto it first thing in the morning. In the meantime, you can decide where you want to eat while I have a shower.'

'Right here,' she said. 'It will be ready by the time you are. Baked trout, and all the trimmings, followed by strawberry shortcake. Bought, I'm afraid. I've never tried my hand at cake-making. One of the things I'm going to have plenty of time to experiment with these next few months.'

It was evident that Zac had registered the edge she couldn't quite eradicate from her voice, but he let it pass. If they were going to make this work, it had to be an all-out effort, Jessica chided herself as he departed for the shower. The break he'd suggested was a good start. They might even manage to recapture some of the zest they'd known together in the beginning.

Apart from something of a contretemps over her refusal to abandon the doctor she'd already seen twice in favour of the Harley Street gynaecologist who would have been Zac's choice, the evening passed without incident. Spending too many like this wasn't going to help the situation, though, Jessica reflected, sensing restlessness on his part. He was accustomed to being out and about of an evening, not sitting around. There was no reason why she should be restricted in any way herself as yet, of course. She had to make the most of the next few weeks while she still retained some semblance of a figure.

The memory of what Zac had said about some men finding pregnancy a sexual turn-off returned to haunt her later when they made love for the first time in over a week. Hard as she tried to persuade herself that she was imagining it, she sensed a certain holding back on Zac's part. If it affected him already when there was no discernible alteration in her shape, how was it going to be later when she lost it altogether? she wondered bleakly.

They flew out to the Hawaiian islands the following Monday, breaking the journey with a two-night stopover in Los Angeles. Jessica found the vast, sprawling city overwhelming, the traffic murderous, the daytime heat enervating. The best part was the concert they attended at Hollywood Bowl. Seated under a starlit sky, ears filled with glorious sound, she felt thoroughly uplifted.

'Wonderful!' she exclaimed on the way back to their hotel when Zac asked how she'd enjoyed it. 'You'll have been before, of course?'

'Only once,' he returned. 'LA isn't one of my favourite places. You'll find Maui an oasis of peace after this. Sand, sea and wonderful scenery!'

'It sounds idyllic.' Jessica could hardly wait to get there. 'I'm still finding the whole thing hard to take in,' she confessed. 'The farthest I've been before this is Greece. I'd never in a million years have imagined being here!'

'There's a lot more world out there.' Zac sounded easy. 'We're only scratching the surface. New Zealand is well worth a visit. Australia too—providing you're not scared of spiders.'

'Whoa!' Jessica was laughing. 'I can't take too much in at once!' She sobered a little to add, 'Did you tell anyone yet?'

'About the baby?' He shook his head, expression giving

little away. 'Time enough when we get back. You'll still be under the three-month mark.'

She'd be beginning to show definite signs at twelve weeks, Jessica reflected. The waistband of the skirt she was wearing felt tighter than normal already. She'd packed only one-piece bathing suits. Bikinis were way too revealing.

The freeway was thronged, cars changing lanes from either side with scant attention to the proximity of other vehicles. Zac handled the hire car with his customary confidence. He looked wonderful in the cream jacket and dark blue open-necked shirt. Judging from the feminine glances turned their way tonight, she wasn't the only one to think so. Something she had to learn to accept, because it was certainly going to keep on happening.

It would be no problem if she were sure of his feelings for her, she acknowledged. She could even enjoy the attention he drew—bask in the envy. Only she wasn't, and never would be unless he laid it on the line, and that was unlikely given the way things were. She could put him in his grandfather's good books, but she couldn't make him love her the way she wanted him to.

Maui was a dream island, its verdant green heights enclosing lush inland valleys, its coastline ringed by inlets and coves. Above all towered the twin volcanos, extinct now but still spectacular.

Zac chartered a helicopter to take them up on a soaring, zooming ride over the Haleakala crater. To Jessica, the whole experience was breathtaking.

'I feel like Alice in Wonderland!' she exclaimed, almost reluctant to have her feet on the ground again. 'England's going to seem pretty tame after all this.'

'You'll have plenty to keep you occupied when we get back,' Zac rejoined. 'Babies need a lot of things. I don't think the mews is the ideal place for a child either. We should start looking for somewhere more suited.'

'You'd hate to lose the cottage,' Jessica protested. 'You know you would.'

His shrug was dismissive. 'I daresay I could cope with it. We could even keep it as a *pied à terre*.'

'This baby is changing your whole life,' she said ruefully.

He gave a dry smile. 'Not nearly as much as it's going to change yours. Men have the easy part.' He viewed her face under the shading straw hat, gaze dropping momentarily to the already reinforced swell of her breasts against the thin cotton of her shirt. 'Let's get back to the hotel,' he added on a suddenly roughened note.

The love-making was intense from both sides. Jessica revelled in the passionate, uninhibited caresses. Holding the dark head nestled at her breast afterwards, she allowed herself a cautious optimism. Just because his father had found the later stages of pregnancy a turn-off, it didn't *have* to follow that Zac would. Even if he did, assuming that he'd follow in his father's footsteps and seek solace elsewhere was doing him an injustice. If she loved him, she had to put some trust in him.

The following days were idyllic. They swam in the sea, lazed on the beach, spent the evenings dining and dancing under the stars. The hotel was old Colonial, surrounded by wide verandas and cooled by huge wicker ceiling fans rather than modern air-conditioning. Jessica loved the place.

Morning sickness a thing of the past, she found her hair and skin blooming, her eyes taking on an added sparkle. Zac himself was moved to comment on her vitality.

'Just don't overdo it,' he said one morning when she emerged breathless but exhilarated from a session of water aerobics in the hotel pool. 'This is supposed to be a rest.'

'There'll be plenty of time for that later when I'm car-rying all before me,' she responded blithely, regretting the turn of phrase immediately in its reminder of how she was going to look in another two or three months. 'How's the book?' she added, busying herself with the towel.

'Not exactly riveting,' he admitted. 'I thought we might take a drive over to Hana on the east coast this afternoon.'

It was obvious that he was bored. Jessica couldn't blame him. He was unaccustomed to taking things easy. 'Good idea,' she said. 'It would be a shame to come all this way and just stick around the hotel and beach.'

Concentrating on her towelling, she could still see him on the periphery of her vision. Laid out on the lounger, clad only in brief white trunks that outlined his masculin-ity, he was enough to set any woman's pulses racing. The voluptuous redhead seated nearby was certainly paying him enough attention.

Zac would have noticed her, of course. No man with normal reflexes could fail to notice her. Jessica hadn't seen her around the place before, which suggested a recent arrival. She appeared to be alone.

A mistaken impression she found a moment later when the woman was joined by a man unmistakably known to her. Older by a good twenty years, though not unattractive in a swarthy kind of way, he sat down on the edge of her lounger to lean over and kiss her, one hand seeking the swell of her breast beneath the scanty bikini top without care for any observers. The woman gave a laugh and drew him closer, sliding the tips of her fingers teasingly beneath the waistband of his trunks.

Jessica looked hastily away. That kind of behaviour in public was reprehensible! Zac was reading again, and seemed unaware of what was going on, though he only had to lift his eyes. Whether he, as a man, would view the scene with the same aversion was open to question. He might even be turned on by it himself.

She moved with deliberation to block his view if he did glance up. If anyone was going to turn him on, it would be her! Only certainly not here.

'I think I'll go up and wash my hair before lunch,' she murmured.

'Fine.' Despite what he'd said about the book a few minutes ago, it certainly seemed to be holding his attention now. 'See you later, then.'

Short of rescinding on the hair-washing idea, Jessica had no choice other than to leave him there. Offered a similar incentive only yesterday, he hadn't hesitated, but even the most enjoyable of pastimes could pall if too readily available. It was time she held back a little—left it to him to make the running. It was playing games, but if that was what it took to keep his interest alive, then so be it.

She had her hair washed and dried by the time he came up to the room to change. He took a shower himself to get rid of the sun lotion, emerging from the bathroom nude to find fresh underwear.

'I fixed up a car for this afternoon,' he said, pulling on a pair of boxer shorts. 'We could have dinner out for a change.'

'As good as a rest,' Jessica agreed lightly. 'How long were you planning on staying here, anyway?'

Grey eyes sought green through the mirror where she was putting the finishing touches to her hair, expression hard to read from this distance. 'Had enough, have you?'

'I thought you might have,' she said.

His shrug was brief. 'I can stand a few more days, though it doesn't have to be here. We can move to Oahu, if you like. Or Hawaii itself.'

'Or go home?' she suggested, reading between the lines. 'I'm ready if you are.'

'Fair enough.' He turned away to select a shirt and light cotton trousers from the wardrobe. 'I'll check the flight situation.'

It might be a day or two before seats were available, Jessica consoled herself, already regretting the gesture.

The drive to Hana on the east coast was one of soaring vistas, winding along the ocean past isolated fishing villages, weaving inland through lush groves of mango and dense jungle growth. Waterfalls cascaded everywhere.

She could quite happily settle here, Jessica acknowledged. She would certainly be sorry to leave it all behind to return to city life and English weather. There had been a time when the idea of living in London had held a great deal of appeal, but not any longer. Much as she loved it, the mews cottage itself was going to seem confining after this.

Zac appeared to have forgotten about eating out. They were back at the hotel by seven. Jessica put on a dress he had bought her in LA. Ankle length, and softly flowing in a greeny gold that lit highlights in her hair, it was the most expensive garment she had ever owned. Zac's approving scrutiny gave her a much needed boost.

'Definitely you,' he said.

He was wearing the lightweight cream jacket over dark green trousers and shirt himself. They made, Jessica had to admit, a good-looking pair. She would willingly have forsworn dinner in favour of an early night, but she kept the notion to herself.

The couple she'd noted in the morning took the table next to them in the restaurant. Flamboyant in a red that exactly toned with her hair, her hour-glass figure shown to its best advantage by the body hugging design of her dress, the woman drew every male eye in the place.

'I overheard you saying you were going to drive over

to Hana this afternoon?' she said to Zac as she took her seat. 'Would you recommend it?'

'I think you'd find it well worth the effort,' he returned easily.

'Oh, good! I'm Corinne, by the way,' she added. 'And this is Ralph.'

Jessica fastened a smile to her lips as Zac responded in the same informal vein, already anticipating the other woman's suggestion that the four of them join forces for dinner. If she'd wanted company at all, they were the last people she would have chosen.

She had no reason to change her mind on that score as the evening wore on. Ralph was loud in every sense of the word, with a brand of humour she found too coarse to be amusing. As for Corinne herself, it was obvious from the word go where *her* interests lay. Not that Zac appeared reluctant to bear the brunt.

The two were here in Maui as part of a tour organised by Orbis, it turned out. The discovery that Zac was a director of the company stimulated Corinne even further. She was his for the asking, thought Jessica cynically, no stranger herself to the desire openly expressed in the woman's eyes.

Zac's expression gave no hint of his feelings, though he could hardly fail to be aware of the offer. Neither could Ralph, but if he felt any resentment he certainly wasn't showing it. His suggestion that the four of them might consider changing partners for the night came as an utter shock—to Jessica, at any rate. She left no one in any doubt of *her* feelings on the matter by getting abruptly to her feet and walking away.

Zac caught up with her as she headed for the privacy of their suite. 'A simple no would have been sufficient,' he said mildly, falling into step.

'For you, perhaps,' she returned, still churning inside

at the very thought. 'If no was the answer *you* had in mind.'

His laugh was short. 'You reckon I was tempted?'

'Weren't you?' she challenged, still without looking at him. 'You've made it pretty obvious that you find Corinne an eyeful.'

'She's all of that,' he said. 'As most men back there tonight would agree. That doesn't mean I had any thoughts about spending the night with her.'

'But you wouldn't have turned the chance down if you'd been on your own.'

'The chance probably wouldn't have been offered if I'd been on my own. Those two work as a pair.'

They had reached the door to their suite. Jessica opened it with the key she had ready in her hand and went inside, waiting to close the door again as Zac passed her by.

'They're utter trash!' she burst out. 'Both of them! They should be locked up!'

She hadn't switched on any lights. Standing with his back to the windows, Zac's face was in shadow. 'For what?' he asked. 'They're doing nothing against the law. People get their kicks in different ways.'

'You mean you see nothing wrong in that kind of behaviour yourself?'

'You're putting words in my mouth.' The tolerance was beginning to sound distinctly strained. 'It's been a long day. You're tired, and overreacting. Let's just forget the whole thing and get some sleep.'

Jessica bit back the words trembling on her lips as he turned to head for the bedroom. Telling him sleep was the only thing he *was* going to get tonight might call forth an answer she didn't want to hear. It was best, she knew, to do as he said and put the whole episode from mind, but not so easy to effect. She could hardly avoid any further contact at all with Corinne and Ralph while they were all staying in the same hotel.

Zac was in the shower when she finally followed him through to the bedroom. Most nights she would have joined him. Tonight she waited for him to finish, using the time to start collecting things together.

He was nude but for a towel slung about his hips when he emerged from the bathroom. The hair on his chest still bore traces of moisture in tiny beads that sparkled in the lamplight.

'Going somewhere?' he asked as she dumped a pile of clothing into the suitcase she had opened on the stand.

'You said you'd try for a flight out in the morning,' Jessica reminded him. 'I thought it best to be prepared.'

'There'll be time enough to pack when we have a flight arranged,' he said. 'It might be a couple of days.'

'In which case, I'd prefer to spend them at another hotel.'

'Because of those two downstairs?'

His tone drew her head up. The colour high in her cheeks, she met the impatient grey regard. 'It might not be reason enough for you, but it's more than enough for me! Sorry if it robs you of the opportunity to feast your eyes on Corinne's luscious curves, but life is full of disappointments.'

Zac stretched a sardonic smile. 'Isn't it just? There was a time…' He broke off, shaking his head as if in rejection of what he'd been about to say. 'All right, I'll see to it. Leave that for now. It can be done in the morning.'

He went over to the bed, discarding the towel to slide between the smooth cotton sheets. With the memory of Corinne's voluptuous figure still prominent in her mind's eye, Jessica risked no comparisons by undressing in the bedroom in front of him.

Through in the luxurious bathroom, she stripped off,

faced with a multi image of herself in the mirror-lined walls. Her waist was definitely thicker, her belly already acquiring some slight curvature. Secure in the love of the man she had married, she could have viewed the changes in her shape with a totally different attitude. As it was, she saw them only the way she was sure he would see them. How long would he continue to want her?

She had the answer to that question when she went back to the bedroom to find him already asleep. The beginning, she thought hollowly, of the end.

CHAPTER ELEVEN

THEY flew back to LA two days later, to London the day after that.

It was coming up to eight o'clock in the evening when they finally reached home. Zac must have contacted the agency at some point to say when they would be back, because there was fresh food in the house that could only have been brought in by Barbara.

'There'll be time enough for that tomorrow,' Zac declared when Jessica made a move to start unpacking the suitcases after they'd eaten. 'What we both need right now is a good night's sleep. I'll take the guest room so we don't disturb one another.'

Not for anything, Jessica silently vowed, was she going to let him see how much that hurt her. 'Good idea,' she said. 'Although I doubt if *anything* would disturb me.'

It was apparent from the spark momentarily lighting the grey eyes that the intimation hadn't been lost on him, but he made no comment. They went upstairs together, parting on the landing with a kiss that left everything to be desired.

Jessica found sleep hard to come by, weary though she was. It was four days since Zac had last made love to her. Four days during which he had shown her every consideration except the one she so desperately needed. She could try making an approach herself, of course, but she knew she wouldn't. The move had to come from him: proof that he still found her desirable at all.

He must have fetched fresh clothing from the bedroom while she was in the shower, because he was already

164

dressed and finishing his breakfast when she got down.

'I'm going in to the office,' he said. 'There's going to be a hell of a lot to catch up on.'

You were the one who suggested the trip, Jessica felt like telling him. She refrained because it was pointless.

'Sure to be,' she said. 'I've plenty to do myself, sorting everything out.'

'I imagine so.' His tone was dry. 'You don't have to lose yourself in domesticity. Barbara will be coming in tomorrow as usual. Take it easy. Put your feet up with a coffee and a magazine.'

'I'm pregnant, not paralysed!' she retorted shortly. '*I'll* decide what I can or can't tackle!'

'Fair enough.' He was obviously making an effort to be reasonable. 'I'll leave you to it, then.'

His parting kiss was brief. A duty done, in Jessica's estimation. Still not in the least bit hungry, but mindful of the life growing inside her, she forced down a couple of pieces of toast and marmalade. If nothing else went right, the baby wasn't going to suffer.

With the unpacking finished, she made herself a coffee and took it out onto the little balcony opening off the main bedroom to drink it in the sunshine. They were lucky, she supposed, to have landed back in the middle of one of Britain's finer periods.

The courtyard was ablaze with colour from the summer flowers festooning every available surface. She'd seen little so far of their neighbours. The people who lived at numbers three and four rarely seemed to be at home at all, while the two youngish men sharing number one kept themselves very much to themselves. All the same, she would miss the place if Zac kept to his plan to find somewhere out of the city to live, though she had to agree that

a house in the country would offer a great deal more freedom to a child.

That she and Zac would still be together when the baby
was born she didn't doubt for a moment. Even without
his grandfather's attitude to consider, he wasn't the type
to walk away from responsibility of that nature. What kind
of marriage it would be by then she hesitated to imagine.
Love she might manage to do without if she had to, but
minus even passion...

The phone call from Esther Prescott came around noon.

'Zac rang to tell us the news!' exclaimed the older
woman. 'I can't tell you how happy we both are for you!
You must come down to see us again, Jessica. I know
you've only just come back from America, but you could
manage a weekend before too long, couldn't you?'

'Of course we could.' There was little else Jessica could
say. 'How about this weekend?' she suggested, giving
way to the inevitable. 'We can travel down tomorrow
night.'

'That would be absolutely lovely! If you're sure you're
not going to be too tired after your trip.'

'I'm fine,' Jessica assured her. 'Tomorrow it is then.'

She'd no sooner put the phone down than it rang again.
Leonie sounded aggrieved. 'I've been trying to contact
you for days! Your office said you'd left. Where the devil
have you been?'

Until this moment, Jessica had forgotten all about her
cousin. She barely knew what to say to her now.

'Zac took me to Hawaii,' she responded. 'We only got
back last night.'

'Lucky you!' There was a pause, a change of tone. 'So
everything is going well with the two of you?'

Jessica brightened her own tone. 'Oh, wonderful! I'm
pregnant.'

'Really?' From the sound of it, Leonie was totally non-plussed. 'Intentionally?'

'No,' Jessica admitted. 'Accidents will happen even in this day and age. But I'm happy about it. We both are. It's what marriage is about, after all.'

'Not everyone would agree with you, but someone has to keep the race going. Congratulations, anyway. How about coming over for dinner Saturday?'

'Can we make it next week? We're in Dorset this week-end.'

'To see the great-grandparents-to-be? They must be thrilled by the news.'

'I'm sure they are, although they already have one great-grandchild courtesy of Zac's…cousin, of course.' Jessica had almost said brother. 'There's someone at the door,' she lied, unable to keep up the act any longer. 'I'll ring you Monday and arrange something.'

It was relief to get off the phone. Leonie was no fool; she'd probably already gleaned that all wasn't quite as it should be. Hopefully, she would put any edginess she'd picked up on down to hormonal changes.

Zac got in at seven. From his lack of surprise on hearing they would be travelling down to Dorset the following evening, Jessica could only assume he'd anticipated as much.

He ate the mixed grill she had prepared with every evidence of enjoyment. She stuck to salmon salad for herself, and had difficulty finishing even that.

'When are you due to see the doctor again?' Zac asked, watching her pick listlessly at the fish.

'I start ante-natal clinic the week after next,' she said. 'I suppose I'll be seeing him then.'

'*We'll* be seeing him,' came the steady response. The dark brows lifted as hers drew sharply together. 'It's the done thing these days, I believe, for the father to share as much of the experience as is possible.'

'But not mandatory,' she rejoined. 'I'll be fine on my own.'

'I daresay you would, but I'm still going to be there. All the way through.'

Green eyes took on a faint spark. 'Getting one up on Brady?'

'If that's the way you want to see it. I prefer to view it as a responsibility.'

Looking across the table at the firm male features, Jessica felt her antagonism melt. He was assuming a role totally outside his nature. The least she could do was meet him halfway.

'Sorry,' she proffered. 'That was uncalled for.'

He smiled briefly. 'We all say things off the top at times. I haven't thanked you yet for agreeing to this weekend. I know how you feel about my grandfather.'

Without whose input she wouldn't even be here, came the thought. 'What's done is done,' she said. 'There's no point being angry about it any more. All we can do is make the best of what we've finished up with.'

Expression unrevealing, he inclined his head. 'As you say.'

They spent the following couple of hours or so in what for any normal relationship could have passed as marital contentment, watching a nature programme on television, listening to some music, chatting about this and that. Pleasant enough though it was on the surface, by ten-thirty Jessica was all out of make-believe.

'I think I'll go on up,' she said.

'I think it's time we both did,' Zac responded. 'Jet-lag can last a few days—especially after flying west to east.'

An excuse to spend yet another night sleeping separately, Jessica took it. She preceded him up the stairs, scarcely knowing what she felt when he made no attempt to say goodnight on the landing the way he'd done the night before. If he made love to her tonight it would prove that the physical desire still existed, but how long was that alone going to last?

It made no difference once he took hold of her. There could be no pretence from his side, of course: he was fully aroused before she even touched him. He took it gently at first, but it wasn't gentleness she needed after six starved nights. She wrapped her legs about his hips, urging him deeper, faster, until he lost all control and loosed the flooding warmth she craved.

It was several minutes before he stirred. 'And there I was thinking I was doing you a service by not making any demands,' he murmured against her shoulder.

'What gave you that impression?' Jessica asked carefully.

'Your whole attitude toward me these past few days. I thought you might be going through another of those phases you mentioned.' His voice took on a wry note. 'It's impossible for a man to have any real concept of what a woman does go through in pregnancy.'

'It's going to get worse before it gets better,' she said with masochistic purpose. 'I'm going to be putting on weight—swelling up like a balloon!'

The pause seemed to stretch to infinity. When he did speak it was without inflection. 'But worth it in the end.'

So far as the baby itself was concerned, Jessica could agree. If nothing else, she'd have that to sustain her.

The drive to Dorset took more than four hours due to a storm. Saturday morning brought little change in the weather, with the whole weekend forecast depressing.

'Such a pity it had to choose *this* weekend to change,'

lamented Esther. 'There's so little for you to do down here when it rains.'

'You can give me a game of chess, Zac,' declared her husband. 'You women can enjoy yourselves talking babies,' he added on an indulgent note. 'Just providing you do it out of earshot. Chess calls for concentration.'

The kind no mere woman could be expected to apply, Jessica assumed. She controlled the retort that rose to her lips with an effort, sensing Esther's silent appeal.

'Thank you for holding back just now,' said the latter when the two of them were alone in the conservatory with its deep and comfortable armchairs. 'Henry sees men and women as having their own particular roles in life, that's all.'

'Something you accept yourself?' Jessica felt moved to ask.

'Something I was brought up to accept. It's been a small enough price to pay for all he's given me in other ways over the years. He was a rock when we lost our sons.'

'It must have been devastating for you both,' Jessica said softly. 'Even more so when you got to know whose son Brady really was.'

Esther let out her breath on a sigh. 'So you know about that.'

'Zac told me, yes.'

'Well, right enough. There should be no secrets between husband and wife. It would have saved a lot of heartache all round if Brady's mother had kept the affair to herself, but she chose not to. Needless to say, she's no longer regarded as a member of the Prescott family. Isabel must be delighted. I take it you've spoken with her?'

'Yesterday,' Jessica confirmed. 'And she is.'

'She deserves some happiness after what she must have gone through all those years knowing what she knew.

Howard was very fortunate to have a wife who would not only stay with him, but make it appear that everything was normal between them. If Henry had ever guessed the truth…' She broke off, shaking her head. 'All in the past. We have a whole new generation to look to. I imagine Zac would like a boy too.'

Dulcie's arrival with coffee saved Jessica from finding a reply. She had no idea what Zac's preference would be, nor any intention of asking. She still had to come to terms with the fact that she was having a baby at all.

The rain continued throughout the day, and for most of the night, giving way to a near gale force wind that sprang up around dawn. It was hardly the weather for it, Henry objected, when Jessica suggested that she and Zac take a walk after breakfast. In any case, they were here to spend time as a family, not to go gallivanting over the country-side. Zac could give him another game of chess this morning.

He made it difficult, Jessica had to admit, for Zac to refuse without being downright uncivil, but she still resented the fact that he made no attempt. It was high time *someone* stood up to the old devil. He'd had his way for far too long.

The antipathy built in her as the day progressed, reaching fusion point shortly before they left, when Henry told her he'd instructed Zac to book an appointment with a Harley Street gynaecologist.

'I can't think what he was about letting you go to an ordinary GP to start with!' he declared.

'It was *my* choice,' Jessica answered tautly. 'It still is. You might be able to dictate to everyone else, but you're not doing it with me!'

He eyed her for a lengthy moment, obviously and thoroughly taken aback. When he did speak it was with some reserve. 'I'll put that little outburst down to your condition. Women tend to become over-emotional at these times.'

'What would you know about it?' she demanded. 'What interest did you ever take in anyone but yourself and what *you* want? You'd even lie to get your own way! Not only that, but you force your wife to lie too!' She had the bit between her teeth now, the bitterness and resentment of the past weeks driving her on. 'You really enjoy wielding power, don't you? Keeping control of the company— playing your grandsons off against one another. If you had any real feeling for them at all, you'd give them their dues now rather than hold the will over their heads for the next how ever many years!'

She did stop there, deflation setting in fast. Henry appeared more stunned than angry at the moment, but that wasn't likely to last. She resisted the impulse to try apologising because she couldn't bring herself to regret anything she had said. Not yet, at any rate. She turned abruptly and left him.

Zac had been to take their bags out to the car. She ran into him in the hall on his return to the house.

'What happened?' he asked shrewdly.

'I just gave your grandfather a few well-deserved home truths,' Jessica admitted, wiping any element of defensiveness from her voice. 'I think we might both of us be *persona non grata* from now on. Me for my lippy mouth, you for your failure to put me in my place!'

The hint of amusement in the curve of Zac's lips was a surprise. 'Sounds about right on both counts,' he said.

Jessica gazed at him in silence for a moment, the wind taken completely from her sails. 'Doesn't it bother you that I might have made him angry enough to cut you from his will?'

'I've had that threat hanging over me for years. I daresay I'd cope if it happened.'

'Even if it meant Brady gaining the upper hand?'

He shrugged briefly, eyes veiled again. 'We're probably talking several years more before that becomes an issue. I've other things to think about.'

Such as a marriage that should never have taken place, and a baby tying him to it, came the wry thought. Tying them both to it, in fact.

Esther came through from the kitchen where she had been preparing vegetables for the evening meal in Dulcie's absence. 'About ready for off, are you?' she said. 'I think Henry's in the sitting room.'

'I doubt if he'll be in any mood to wave us goodbye,' said Jessica, this time allowing a certain ruefulness to creep into her voice. 'I'm afraid I let my temper run away with me just now.'

Esther gave a sigh. 'I've been expecting it all weekend.'

'I'll go and see him.' Zac was moving as he spoke. 'Wait for me in the car, Jess.'

Esther accompanied her outdoors. 'You won't let this stop you from visiting again, will you?' she asked anxiously.

'I don't imagine *I'm* going to be very welcome,' Jessica returned. 'Zac neither, unless he can convince his grandfather he's capable of bringing me to heel.'

Esther had to smile. 'I doubt if he has any intention of trying. Unlike my husband—and Brady too, to a certain extent—Zac doesn't see women as in any way the secondary sex. He'll stand up for you.'

If he had, he'd received short shrift, Jessica reflected as he emerged from the house. Not that he looked concerned.

They were well on their way before she ventured to ask what his grandfather had said.

'Surprisingly little,' he acknowledged. 'He seemed quite subdued, in fact. You might even have given him food for thought.'

Some hope, she thought. Eighty years of male chauvinism wasn't going to be overcome by a few words.

'What exactly was it that sparked you off, anyway?' Zac asked after a moment.

'He said he'd instructed you to make an appointment with a Harley Street gyno.' Jessica slanted a glance. 'Is it true?'

'True that he said it, yes.'

'And were you going to?'

His lips twisted. 'You already made your views quite clear on that score. It was simply easier to go along with him. And yes, I agree, we've all probably done a deal too much going along over the years—or appearing to. If I hadn't tried fobbing him off with a non-existent fiancée in the first place...'

He broke off, applying brakes and swerving as some animal darted across the road in front of them. The comment was left hanging, but Jessica knew what he'd been about to say. If he hadn't lied himself they wouldn't be in this situation to start with. He wasn't the only one with regrets.

The week crawled by. Zac hadn't mentioned moving again, and Jessica had scant interest in pursuing the subject herself. At least here in the city she was within reasonably easy reach of everything—hospitals included. After Sarah's experience, she certainly wouldn't want to be far away.

Reluctant to spend an afternoon with Barbara in the house, she visited her sister-in-law on the Wednesday. Richard had altered considerably in just the few short weeks since she had last seen him. His eyes, she noted, were already more grey than blue.

Holding him, she felt the first real stirring of mother love for the infant developing inside her. In a few months she would be cuddling her own child. Boy or girl it didn't matter.

'So I was right when I thought you might be pregnant too!' Sarah chortled delightedly, having already heard the news from Brady.

'Feminine instinct.' Jessica smiled back. 'I don't imagine Brady's quite as happy about it.'

'Oh, he can still claim kudos with his grandfather for being the first to produce—even more so if yours and Zac's turns out to be a girl. Henry's a chauvinist through and through!'

'I know.' Jessica hesitated before asking. 'Have you spoken with Esther recently?'

'Brady rang Monday night. He thought she sounded a bit strained—though who wouldn't after sixty years of life with a superior being! I'd love to be a fly on the wall the day she finally lets go and gives him what for! Not that I really see it happening. She's left it a bit too late to join the feminist movement.'

Considering what the older woman had said on Sunday, Jessica had to agree. It was obvious there had been no mention made of her own letting go, but that didn't mean it had been passed over by the recipient. There was every possibility that Henry had already taken steps to sideline the grandson who couldn't even teach his wife to show proper respect.

Barbara had left when she got back at four, but there was a message waiting for her on the machine. Zac had gone trouble-shooting up north again.

He'd been home to collect some things: the suit he'd been wearing that morning was lying on the bed. Looking at it, thinking of the long lonely evening ahead, Jessica knew a sudden surging rejection. She couldn't live life this way, trapped in a marriage based on so little. She had to get away. Right away!

She had never returned the key to Leonie's apartment in Majorca, she remembered. With any luck, she could get a flight out tonight.

She gave herself no time to consider. A phone call to the airport confirmed a seat available on a flight leaving at a quarter to eight. By six o'clock she was in a taxi heading out to Heathrow. She left no message—no indication at all of where she had gone.

Majorcan nights in mid June were vastly hotter than they had been in April. Reality kicked in when the only car available for hire without prior reservation proved to be a little Fiat with no air-conditioning. Jessica drove the whole way to the apartment with all the windows down, but still arrived there feeling like a limp rag.

Apart from a flimsy scarf draped across a chair arm, the place was as she had left it all those weeks ago. Prior to this moment, she hadn't given a thought to the possibility of Leonie turning up. Something that would have to be handled if and when. Right now, it was sleep she needed.

Physically and emotionally exhausted, she went out like a light the minute her head touched the pillow, waking to sunlight with no recollection for a moment of where she was.

Depression swamped her as memory returned, along with the rationality that had been missing last night. How could she have imagined that walking out on her marriage was any solution? Zac was hardly going to accept it. Not with the baby on the way. All she'd done was make things even worse than they'd been to start with.

For a moment she wondered if it might be possible to get back before he even knew she had gone, but rationality knocked that notion on the head too. Even if she could get a flight this morning, it was unlikely that he wouldn't have attempted to contact her.

The only reasonable thing she could do now was telephone him and tell him where she was. He would be furious, and rightly so; he'd made every effort to sustain the marriage; far more than she had herself. So the time might come when he stopped wanting her. She would just have to deal with it. The baby took precedence.

Rolling to sit up, she caught sight of the clock on the bedside table, shocked to find it was already a quarter to ten. Hardly so surprising though, she supposed, considering it had been coming up to two in the morning when she got to bed.

She donned a negligée Leonie had left in the wardrobe, running an automatic hand through the tumble of chestnut hair as she passed a mirror. She needed a drink to ease the dryness in her throat before making the call. Procrastination, she knew, but a few minutes wasn't going to make any difference.

It was more like half an hour and two coffees later when she finally got round to dialling the Chelsea number. Apart from Zac's voice on the answering machine, there was no reply. His mobile was switched off too. Jessica contemplated leaving a message on the latter, but she couldn't find the right words—if there were any right words in a situation like this.

The hard knock on the outer door jerked every nerve in her body. The caretaker come to see who was in the apartment at a time when the owner almost certainly wouldn't be, she surmised. She went reluctantly to answer the summons, staring in stunned silence at the all-too-familiar figure on the landing.

Wearing a suit that looked as if it had been slept in, jawline in need of a shave, Zac regarded her hardily.

'Are you going to invite me in?' he asked.

Jessica stood back to allow him free passage, closing the door and leaning against it for support against the weakness in her lower limbs.

'How did you know where I was?' she managed.

'I drove back after phoning three times last night and failing to get a reply,' he said. 'I saw some of your things were gone, and took it that you'd done a runner. The last outgoing call shown on the telephone display was to the airport. It didn't take a genius, once I'd discovered which flight you were on, to work out where you'd be. I managed to get a seat on a six-thirty charter flight out of Gatwick.' He paused, drawing a harsh breath, the anger breaking through at last. 'What the hell happened to make you go to these lengths?'

'Nothing *happened*,' she said huskily. 'I just had to get away, that's all.'

'From what? Me?'

Jessica made an effort to pull herself together. 'From the whole sorry mess.'

His jaw contracted. 'Including the baby?'

Her eyes flared emerald bright as his meaning sank in. 'You really think I'm capable of getting rid of it?'

'I'm not sure,' he admitted. 'Knowing how far from happy you are to be pregnant at all.'

'That's not true!'

'No?' Zac studied her with a certain cynicism. 'You can honestly claim to be over the moon about it?'

Jessica swallowed thickly. The truth, the whole truth, and nothing but the truth from now on, she vowed. 'If I'm not, it isn't because of the baby itself. You said once that men find pregnancy a sexual turn-off.'

'I said *some* men,' he rejoined. 'If I gave you the impression I included myself in there, it certainly wasn't intentional. I'm not going to try making out that I'm drawn to pregnant women in general, but there's a hell of a difference when it's a personal involvement.'

'I'm only just beginning to show,' she said, twisting the knife. 'You reckon you'll still want to make love to me when I blow up like a beached whale?'

A glimmer of humour sprang in the grey eyes. 'Something of an exaggeration, I think.' He regarded her reflectively. 'Is sex so all-important to you?'

'No more than it is to you,' she defended. 'What else do we have in common?'

'Enough to carry on with.' His voice had roughened again. 'I realise your feelings for me are far more limited than mine for you right now, but that can change in time. I won't give up on you, Jess!'

It was several moments before she could find her voice, not wholly believing he could mean what he appeared to mean. 'What makes you so sure *my* feelings are limited?' she asked softly.

He didn't answer immediately, eyes penetrating, expression altering. A couple of steps brought him back to where she stood. She went willingly into his arms.

'How long have you loved me?' she murmured eons later, nestling against the broad shoulder.

Zac kissed her temple where the hair clung damply. 'From the moment I switched on the lamp right here in this bedroom and saw you standing there. Not, that I fully recognised it at the time, I admit. All I knew was I had to see you again.'

'You mean you'd have taken steps even if we hadn't run into one another at the hotel?'

'I'd every intention. I could hardly believe it when I found you sitting at the table that lunchtime.'

'It wasn't the kind of place I'd normally have chosen to lunch at,' Jessica admitted. 'Something drew me.'

'The answer to a prayer in more ways than one. Although asking you to play my fiancée could hardly be called the ideal start to a relationship,' he added ruefully. 'I was lucky to have you say yes.'

Jessica laughed. 'I didn't have the strength of mind to say no. Not with every last part of me clamouring for contact again! Have you any idea how close I came to dragging you right back to bed when you kissed me that night?'

'You wouldn't have had to do much dragging, believe me. I was still wound up from our first contact.'

'You must have known I wasn't Leonie.'

'Not right away. By the time I did realise, I was past doing anything about it. You were so instantly and wonderfully responsive!' He kissed her again. 'I remember thinking this Paul must be quite a guy.'

'He wasn't in the same class. Not in any sense.'

'He must have meant something to you to move in with him.'

Jessica hesitated before replying, searching her mind for the truth. 'I needed someone to care about me. Someone to share my life with. I persuaded myself that Paul was it, even though I knew deep down that he was thoroughly self-centred. I've no doubt he was two-timing me most of the time we were together.'

'If he was, he had no judgement.' Zac's voice was tender. 'You're a very special lady, Mrs Prescott.'

'Who quite likely cost you dear,' she rejoined ruefully. 'Your grandfather is never going to forgive me for what I said to him.'

'I don't know about the forgiveness, but you certainly stirred him. Brady and I learned yesterday morning that he's made over the majority of his shares in the company to the two of us. It came as quite a shock to us both, I can tell you!'

Jessica could hardly believe it herself. 'How will it work out?' she asked tentatively.

'We're both of us going to have to learn how to compromise. We made a start already by burying the hatchet over something we neither of us had a hand in.'

Jessica felt like cheering. 'So Sarah and I can form a proper sister-in-law relationship. I saw her yesterday. I wonder why she didn't mention the shares business?'

'Probably because Brady was saving the news until he got home. The same way I was, until I got called away. I intended telling you when I phoned last night.'

'Except that I wasn't there to tell.' Jessica lifted her head to put her lips to his. 'I was such an idiot, taking off like that. I don't know what I thought it was going to achieve.'

Zac drew her closer still, making her aware of his renewal. 'It brought things to a pitch. How long would we have gone on the way we were, with neither of us prepared to say that one vital word for fear of it not being returned. I was so convinced that you hated being pregnant. That you hated me at times for not taking more care. I didn't plan it, believe me.'

'*I* might have,' she admitted. 'Those times when I forgot to take the Pill could have been deliberate, even if I didn't appreciate it at the time. Freud would have called it a subconscious ploy to tie you to me.'

'Not needed. I was already well and truly hooked.' Zac ran both hands into the cascade of chestnut curls, lifting her face to look into her eyes, his own warm and deep. 'You're not just saying it? You really do want this baby?'

'Totally,' she assured him. 'It's a part of us both. I'm still not looking forward to getting fat though.'

Zac's smile was a reassurance in itself. 'You'll be the loveliest, sexiest mother-to-be that ever was!' The smile faded, the hard-hewn, masculine features taking on an expression that stirred her to the depths. 'I love you, Jess. More than I can find words to tell you. The day you came into my life was the day I really started living.'

'For a man without words, you're doing not at all badly,' she murmured, moved beyond measure by the emotion in his voice. 'I never loved any other man but you. I never could.'

'You'll never have the chance,' he promised. 'Not while I'm alive and kicking, anyway. Till death us do part, we said. That's exactly what it's going to be. No running for the divorce court every time we have a few differences—which we no doubt will, you being such a strong-minded madam.'

Jessica pulled a face at him. 'I need to be now I'm married into the Prescott clan. I'll apologise to your grandfather next time I see him.'

'I wouldn't,' he said. 'He'd take it as a weakness. Who knows, he might even invite you to a game of chess.'

She laughed. 'He'd be very disappointed if he did. I wouldn't even know how to start! Anyway, you men have to have *something* you can do better than we women.'

The grey eyes glinted. 'You reckon a game of chess is it?'

'Well…I suppose there are one or two other things you might get fairly good at, given enough practice. For instance…'

She drew in a shuddering breath as he slid all the way inside her, loving the feel of him, the muscular strength of the arms enclosing her, the sheer possessiveness in his embrace.

A lifetime together wasn't going to be nearly long enough.

EPILOGUE

'THE Prescott genes certainly came through this time,' declared Leonie. 'He looks more like Zac every time I see him!'

Jessica laughed, glancing across the room to where her son sat surrounded by presents he was quite happy to share with his sister and cousins. 'Not just looks either. Even at one, he has a will of iron when he sets his aim on something. Lucy can handle him though.'

'I bet she can.' Leonie directed a fond glance at her pretty, auburn-haired goddaughter who was presently conducting a session of look and learn via one of the books scattered about. 'A born teacher, if ever I saw one! It's hard to believe she's only just five. The apple of her great grandfather's eye too,' she added, turning her gaze in the direction of the elderly couple sitting watching the children. 'Amazing how he's mellowed since she was born.'

'Yes, he was quite off-hand initially because she wasn't a boy, but he came round the first time she singled him out for a smile.' Jessica was smiling herself at the memory. 'It was probably wind, if the truth were known, but it did the trick. He's been utterly besotted ever since. Of course, he's delighted with the boys too. Esther says he talks about little else these days but the grandchildren.'

'Brady still sticking at two?' Leonie queried.

'Not at the last count. Sarah's three months gone.' Jessica lifted a hand in greeting as she caught her sister-in-law's eye. 'She'd like a girl herself this time, but she'll be just as content if it's another boy.'

Leonie chuckled. 'Poor Brady! He didn't stand a chance.'

'Oh, I think he's happy enough with the idea of a large family now. Like his grandfather, he's undergone something of a metamorphosis over the last few years. He and Zac have learned to get along. They even play golf together.'

'You think your move out here to Sevenoaks helped the two of them get to know one another better?'

'I think it helped a great deal. Not that that was the main reason for the move. Sarah and I wanted the children to grow up together. Richard and Lucy are more like brother and sister than cousins, and with Toby barely a year older than Michael, they're a pretty good match too.'

'You'll need to get moving again yourself then, if Sarah's latest isn't to be left out in the cold,' Leonie commented, tongue in cheek. 'What's Zac's view on large families?'

'A philosophical one,' he said, coming up behind the pair of them in time to catch the last. 'I'm happy whatever.'

He slid an arm about Jessica's still slender waist, dropping a light kiss on her cheek. 'Your man of the moment is outside showing signs of family overkill,' he added to Leonie.

'Probably scared to death that I'm heading that way myself,' she said drily. 'I'll go and reassure the poor darling.'

She headed for the door, leaving Jessica with the man who could still send a frisson down her spine with his mere touch: the man she had loved for the last six years, and couldn't imagine life without.

'You think there'll come a time when Leonie meets someone she can visualise a future with?' she murmured.

'Leonie's married to her job,' came the answer. 'She

hasn't the time or inclination for the kind of commitment you're talking about. She never had. Whether she ever will is open to chance.'

Jessica looked up to meet the steady grey eyes, her smile warm. 'You're right, of course. What will be will be. After all, who could have anticipated our future turning out the way it did!'

'Who indeed?' Zac brought up a hand to push a recalcitrant curl from her face, his regard so tender it brought a lump to her throat. 'The luckiest mistake a man ever made!'

Modern Romance™
...seduction and
passion guaranteed

Tender Romance™
...love affairs that
last a lifetime

Sensual Romance™
...sassy, sexy and
seductive

Blaze.
...sultry days and
steamy nights

Medical Romance™
...medical drama on
the pulse

Historical Romance™
...rich, vivid and
passionate

27 new titles every month.

*With all kinds of Romance for
every kind of mood...*

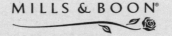

MILLS & BOON®

MILLS & BOON

Winter
weddings

Three brand new Christmas novels

Penny Jordan   Gail Whitiker   Judy Christenberry

Published 18th October 2002

Available at most branches of WH Smith,
Tesco, Martins, Borders, Eason, Sainsbury's
and all good paperback bookshops.

1102/59/SH39

2 FREE

books and a surprise gift!

We would like to take this opportunity to thank you for reading this Mills & Boon® book by offering you the chance to take TWO more specially selected titles from the Modern Romance™ series absolutely FREE! We're also making this offer to introduce you to the benefits of the Reader Service™—

★ FREE home delivery
★ FREE gifts and competitions
★ FREE monthly Newsletter
★ Exclusive Reader Service discount
★ Books available before they're in the shops

Accepting these FREE books and gift places you under no obligation to buy, you may cancel at any time, even after receiving your free shipment. Simply complete your details below and return the entire page to the address below. *You don't even need a stamp!*

YES! Please send me 2 free Modern Romance books and a surprise gift. I understand that unless you hear from me, I will receive 4 superb new titles every month for just £2.55 each, postage and packing free. I am under no obligation to purchase any books and may cancel my subscription at any time. The free books and gift will be mine to keep in any case.

P2ZEA

Ms/Mrs/Miss/Mr ....Initials.....................................
BLOCK CAPITALS PLEASE

Surname ....

Address ....

....

....Postcode.................................

Send this whole page to:
UK: FREEPOST CN81, Croydon, CR9 3WZ
EIRE: PO Box 4546, Kilcock, County Kildare (stamp required)

Offer valid in UK and Eire only and not available to current Reader Service subscribers to this series. We reserve the right to refuse an application and applicants must be aged 18 years or over. Only one application per household. Terms and prices subject to change without notice. Offer expires 31st January 2003. As a result of this application, you may receive offers from Harlequin Mills & Boon and other carefully selected companies. If you would prefer not to share in this opportunity please write to The Data Manager at the address above.

Mills & Boon® is a registered trademark owned by Harlequin Mills & Boon Limited.
Modern Romance™ is being used as a trademark.